A MASTER STORYTELLER FOR ALL TIME...

"Isaac Bashevis Singer writes what Hawthorne called 'romances' rather than novels, and moral fables and allegories rather than short stories.... Singer's subject is *shtetl* (Jewish village) life in Poland... and he brings it into being so powerfully that reading his books one soon comes to believe that our world *is* a fantastic vision."
—*Stanley Edgar Hyman*

"BUT THERE IS ISAAC BASHEVIS SINGER. IF ONLY HE WERE LEFT WRITING IN YIDDISH, IT WOULD STILL BE AN IMPORTANT LITERARY LANGUAGE. HE IS CERTAINLY ONE OF THE MOST REMARKABLE AMERICAN AUTHORS WHO HAS EVER LIVED."
—*Commentary*

Stories translated by
Saul Bellow, Isaac Rosenfeld,
Norbert Guterman, and others

D0051447

Fawcett Crest Books
by Isaac Bashevis Singer:

ISAAC BASHEVIS SINGER

GIMPEL THE FOOL
and other stories

FAWCETT CREST • NEW YORK

GIMPEL THE FOOL

THIS BOOK CONTAINS THE COMPLETE TEXT OF
THE ORIGINAL HARDCOVER EDITION.

Published by Fawcett Crest Books, a unit of CBS Publications, the Consumer Publishing Division of CBS Inc.,
by arrangement with Farrar, Straus & Giroux.

ISBN: 0-449-24275-7

Printed in the United States of America

First Fawcett Crest printing: March 1980

10   9   8   7   6   5   4   3   2   1

ACKNOWLEDGMENTS

These stories were written during the last ten years with the exception of "The Old Man," which appeared in 1933 in Warsaw. Most of them were published in Yiddish in *The Jewish Daily Forward*. All but four have also appeared in English in the following publications: *Partisan Review*, "Gimpel the Fool" and "From the Diary of One Not Born"; *Midstream*, "The Wife Killer"; *Commentary*, "The Gentleman from Cracow" and "Fire"; *New World Writing*, "The Mirror"; *A Treasury of Yiddish Stories*, "The Little Shoemakers" and "Gimpel the Fool." I should like to express my thanks for permission to reprint the stories here. I should also like to thank the editors and translators for their faithful rendering of the originals. In particular my gratitude goes to Elaine Gottlieb, whose assisance in preparing this collection of the stories was invaluable. Finally, I should like to thank the editors of The Noonday Press, Cecil Hemley and Dwight W. Webb, who had the idea for the volume.

CONTENTS

GIMPEL THE FOOL
and other stories

GIMPEL THE FOOL

I

I am Gimpel the Fool. I don't think myself a fool. On the contrary. But that's what folks call me. They gave me the name while I was still in school. I had seven names in all: imbecile, donkey, flax-head, dope, glump, ninny, and fool. The last name stuck. What did my foolishness consist of? I was easy to take in. They said, "Gimpel, you know the rabbi's wife has been brought to childbed?" So I skipped school. Well, it turned out to be a lie. How was I supposed to know? She hadn't had a big belly. But I never looked at her belly. Was that really so foolish? The gang laughed and hee-hawed, stomped and danced and chanted a good-night prayer. And instead of the raisins they give when a woman's lying in, they stuffed my hand full of goat turds. I was no weakling. If I slapped someone he'd see all the way to Cracow. But I'm really not a slugger by nature. I think to myself: Let it pass. So they take advantage of me.

I was coming home from school and heard a dog barking. I'm not afraid of dogs, but of course I never want to start up with them. One of them may be mad, and if he bites there's not a Tartar in the world who can help you. So I made tracks. Then I looked around and saw the whole market place wild with laughter. It was no dog at all but Wolf-Leib the Thief. How was I supposed to know it was he? It sounded like a howling bitch.

When the pranksters and leg-pullers found that I was easy to fool, every one of them tried his luck with me. "Gimpel, the Czar is coming to Frampol; Gimpel, the moon fell down in Turbeen; Gimpel, little Hodel Furpiece found a treasure behind the bathhouse." And I like a golem believed everyone. In the first place, everything is possible, as it is written in the Wisdom of the Fathers, I've forgotten just how. Second, I had to believe when the whole town came down on me! If I ever dared to say, "Ah, you're kidding!" there was trouble. People got angry. "What do you mean! You want to call everyone a liar?" What was I to do? I believed them, and I hope at least that did them some good.

I was an orphan. My grandfather who brought me up was already bent toward the grave. So they turned me over to a baker, and what a time they gave me there! Every woman or girl who came to bake a batch of noodles had to fool me at least once. "Gimpel, there's a fair in heaven; Gimpel, the rabbi gave birth to a calf in the seventh month; Gimpel, a cow flew over the roof and laid brass eggs." A student from the yeshiva came once to buy a roll, and he said,

"You, Gimpel, while you stand here scraping with your baker's shovel the Messiah has come. The dead have arisen." "What do you mean?" I said. "I heard no one blowing the ram's horn!" He said, "Are you deaf?" And all began to cry, "We heard it, we heard!" Then in came Rietze the Candle-dipper and called out in her hoarse voice, "Gimpel, your father and mother have stood up from the grave. They're looking for you."

To tell the truth, I knew very well that nothing of the sort had happened, but all the same, as folks were talking, I threw on my wool vest and went out. Maybe something had happened. What did I stand to lose by looking? Well, what a cat music went up! And then I took a vow to believe nothing more. But that was no go either. They confused me so that I didn't know the big end from the small.

I went to the rabbi to get some advice. He said, "It is written, better to be a fool all your days than for one hour to be evil. You are not a fool. They are the fools. For he who causes his neighbor to feel shame loses Paradise himself." Nevertheless the rabbi's daughter took me in. As I left the rabbinical court she said, "Have you kissed the wall yet?" I said, "No; what for?" She answered, "It's the law; you've got to do it after every visit." Well, there didn't seem to be any harm in it. And she burst out laughing. It was a fine trick. She put one over on me, all right.

I wanted to go off to another town, but then everyone got busy matchmaking, and they were after me so they nearly tore my coat tails off. They talked at me and talked until I got water on the ear. She was no chaste maiden, but they told me she was virgin pure. She had a limp, and they said it was deliberate, from coyness. She had a bastard, and they told me the child was her little brother. I cried, "You're wasting your time. I'll never marry that whore." But they said indignantly, "What a way to talk! Aren't you ashamed of yourself? We can take you to the rabbi and have you fined for giving her a bad name." I saw then that I wouldn't escape them so easily and I thought: They're set on making me their butt. But when you're married the husband's the master, and if that's all right with her it's agreeable to me too. Besides, you can't pass through life unscathed, nor expect to.

I went to her clay house, which was built on the sand, and the whole gang, hollering and chorusing, came after me. They acted like bear-baiters. When we came to the well they stopped all the same. They were afraid to start anything with Elka. Her mouth would open as if it were on a hinge, and she had a fierce tongue. I entered the house. Lines were strung from wall to wall and clothes were drying. Barefoot she stood by the tub, doing the wash. She was dressed in a worn hand-me-down gown of plush. She had her hair put up in braids and pinned across her head. It took my breath away, almost, the reek of it all.

Evidently she knew who I was. She took a look at me and said, "Look who's here! He's come, the drip. Grab a seat."

I told her all; I denied nothing. "Tell me the truth," I said, "are you really a virgin, and is that mischievous Yechiel actually your little brother? Don't be deceitful with me, for I'm an orphan."

"I'm an orphan myself," she answered, "and whoever tries to twist you up, may the end of his nose take a twist. But don't let them think they can take advantage of me. I want a dowry of fifty guilders, and let them take up a collection besides. Otherwise they can kiss my you-know-what." She was very plainspoken. I said, "It's the bride and not the groom who gives a dowry." Then she said, "Don't bargain with me. Either a flat 'yes' or a flat 'no'—Go back where you came from."

I thought: No bread will ever be baked from *this* dough. But ours is not a poor town. They consented to everything and proceeded with the wedding. It so happened that there was a dysentery epidemic at the time. The ceremony was held at the cemetery gates, near the little corpse-washing hut. The fellows got drunk. While the marriage contract was being drawn up I heard the most pious high rabbi ask, "Is the bride a widow or a divorced woman?" And the sexton's wife answered for her, "Both a widow and divorced." It was a black moment for me. But what was I to do, run away from under the marriage canopy?

There was singing and dancing. An old granny danced opposite me, hugging a braided white *chalah*. The master of revels made a "God 'a mercy" in memory of the bride's parents. The schoolboys threw burrs, as on Tishe b'Av fast day. There were a lot of gifts after the sermon: a noodle board, a kneading trough, a bucket, brooms, ladles, household articles galore. Then I took a look and saw two strapping young men carrying a crib. "What do we need this for?" I asked. So they said, "Don't rack your brains about it. It's all right, it'll come in handy." I realized I was going to be rooked. Take it another way though, what did I stand to lose? I reflected: I'll see what comes of it. A whole town can't go altogether crazy.

II

At night I came where my wife lay, but she wouldn't let me in. "Say, look here, is this what they married us for?" I said. And she said, "My monthly has come." "But yesterday they took you to the ritual bath, and that's afterward, isn't it supposed to be?" "Today isn't yesterday," said she, "and yesterday's not today. You can beat it if you don't like it." In short, I waited.

Nor four months later she was in childbed. The townsfolk hid their laughter with their knuckles. But what could I do? She suffered intolerable pains and clawed at the walls. "Gimpel," she cried, "I'm going. Forgive me!" The house filled with women. They were boiling pans of water. The screams rose to the welkin.

The thing to do was to go to the House of Prayer to repeat Psalms, and that was what I did.

The townsfolk liked that, all right. I stood in a corner saying Psalms and prayers, and they shook their heads at me. "Pray, pray!" they told me. "Prayer never made any woman pregnant." One of the congregation put a straw to my mouth and said, "Hay for the cows." There was something to that too, by God!

She gave birth to a boy. Friday at the synagogue the sexton stood up before the Ark, pounded on the reading table, and announced, "The wealthy Reb Gimpel invites the congregation to a feast in honor of the birth of a son." The whole House of Prayer rang with laughter. My face was flaming. But there was nothing I could do. After all, I *was* the one responsible for the circumcision honors and rituals.

Half the town came running. You couldn't wedge another soul in. Women brought peppered chick-peas, and there was a keg of beer from the tavern. I ate and drank as much as anyone, and they all congratulated me. Then there was a circumcision, and I named the boy after my father, may he rest in peace. When all were gone and I was left with my wife alone, she thrust her head through the bed-curtain and called me to her.

"Gimpel," said she, "why are you silent? Has your ship gone and sunk?"

"What shall I say?" I answered. "A fine thing you've done to me! If my mother had known of it she'd have died a second time."

She said, "Are you crazy, or what?"

"How can you make such a fool," I said, "of one who should be the lord and master?"

"What's the matter with you?" she said. "What have you taken it into your head to imagine?"

I saw that I must speak bluntly and openly. "Do you think this is the way to use an orphan?" I said, "You have borne a bastard."

She answered, "Drive this foolishness out of your head. The child is yours."

"How can he be mine?" I argued. "He was born seventeen weeks after the wedding."

She told me then that he was premature. I said, "Isn't he a little too premature?" She said, she had had a grandmother who carried just as short a time and she resembled this grandmother of hers as one drop of water does another. She swore to it with such oaths that you would have believed a peasant at the fair if he had used them. To tell the plain truth, I didn't believe her; but when I talked it over next day with the schoolmaster he told me that the very same thing had happened to Adam and Eve. Two they went up to bed, and four they descended.

"There isn't a woman in the world who is not the granddaughter of Eve," he said.

That was how it was; they argued me dumb. But then, who really knows how such things are?

I began to forget my sorrow. I loved the child madly, and he loved me too. As soon as he saw me he'd wave his little hands and want me to pick him up, and when he was colicky I was the only one who could pacify him. I bought him a little bone teething ring and a little gilded cap. He was forever catching the evil eye from someone, and then I had to run to get one of those abracadabras for him that would get him out of it. I worked like an ox. You know how expenses go up when there's an infant in the house. I don't want to lie about it; I didn't dislike Elka either, for that matter. She swore at me and cursed, and I couldn't get enough of her. What strength she had! One of her looks could rob you of the power of speech. And her orations! Pitch and sulphur, that's what they were full of, and yet somehow also full of charm. I adored her every word. She gave me bloody wounds though.

In the evening I brought her a white loaf as well as a dark one, and also poppyseed rolls I baked myself. I thieved because of her and swiped everything I could lay hands on: ma-

caroons, raisins, almonds, cakes. I hope I may
be forgiven for stealing from the Saturday pots
the women left to warm in the baker's oven. I
would take out scraps of meat, a chunk of pudding, a chicken leg or head, a piece of tripe,
whatever I could nip quickly. She ate and became fat and handsome.

I had to sleep away from home all during the
week, at the bakery. On Friday nights when I
got home she always made an excuse of some
sort. Either she had heartburn, or a stitch in
the side, or hiccups, or headaches. You know
what women's excuses are. I had a bitter time
of it. It was rough. To add to it, this little brother
of hers, the bastard, was growing bigger. He'd
put lumps on me, and when I wanted to hit back
she'd open her mouth and curse so powerfully
I saw a green haze floating before my eyes. Ten
times a day she threatened to divorce me. Another man in my place would have taken French
leave and disappeared. But I'm the type that
bears it and says nothing. What's one to do?
Shoulders are from God, and burdens too.

One night there was a calamity in the bakery; the oven burst, and we almost had a fire.
There was nothing to do but go home, so I went
home. Let me, I thought, also taste the joy of
sleeping in bed in mid-week. I didn't want to
wake the sleeping mite and tiptoed into the
house. Coming in, it seemed to me that I heard
not the snoring of one but, as it were, a double
snore, one a thin enough snore and the other
like the snoring of a slaughtered ox. Oh, I didn't

like that! I didn't like it at all. I went up to the bed, and things suddenly turned black. Next to Elka lay a man's form. Another in my place would have made an uproar, and enough noise to rouse the whole town, but the thought occurred to me that I might wake the child. A little thing like that—why frighten a little swallow, I thought. All right then, I went back to the bakery and stretched out on a sack of flour and till morning I never shut an eye. I shivered as if I had had malaria. "Enough of being a donkey," I said to myself. "Gimpel isn't going to be a sucker all his life. There's a limit even to the foolishness of a fool like Gimpel."

In the morning I went to the rabbi to get advice, and it made a great commotion in the town. They sent the beadle for Elka right away. She came, carrying the child. And what do you think she did? She denied it, denied everything, bone and stone! "He's out of his head," she said. "I know nothing of dreams or divinations." They yelled at her, warned her, hammered on the table, but she stuck to her guns: it was a false accusation, she said.

The butchers and the horse-traders took her part. One of the lads from the slaughterhouse came by and said to me, "We've got our eye on you, you're a marked man." Meanwhile the child started to bear down and soiled itself. In the rabbinical court there was an Ark of the Covenant, and they couldn't allow that, so they sent Elka away.

I said to the rabbi, "What shall I do?"

"You must divorce her at once," said he.

"And what if she refuses?" I asked.

He said, "You must serve the divorce. That's all you'll have to do."

I said, "Well, all right, Rabbi. Let me think about it."

"There's nothing to think about," said he. "You mustn't remain under the same roof with her."

"And if I want to see the child?" I asked.

"Let her go, the harlot," said he, "and her brood of bastards with her."

The verdict he gave was that I mustn't even cross her threshold—never again, as long as I should live.

During the day it didn't bother me so much. I thought: It was bound to happen, the abscess had to burst. But at night when I stretched out upon the sacks I felt it all very bitterly. A longing took me, for her and for the child. I wanted to be angry, but that's my misfortune exactly, I don't have it in me to be really angry. In the first place—this was how my thoughts went— there's bound to be a slip sometimes. You can't live without errors. Probably that lad who was with her led her on and gave her presents and what not, and women are often long on hair and short on sense, and so he got around her. And then since she denies it so, maybe I was only seeing things? Hallucinations do happen. You see a figure or a mannikin or something, but when you come up closer it's nothing, there's not a thing there. And if that's so, I'm doing her an injustice. And when I got so far in my thoughts I started to weep. I sobbed so that I wet the flour where I lay. In the morning I went to the rabbi and told him that I had made a mistake. The rabbi wrote on with his quill, and he said that if that were so he would have to reconsider the whole case. Until he had finished I wasn't to go near my wife, but I might send her bread and money by messenger.

III

Nine months passed before all the rabbis could come to an agreement. Letters went back and forth. I hadn't realized that there could be so much erudition about a matter like this.

Meanwhile Elka gave birth to still another child, a girl this time. On the Sabbath I went to the synagogue and invoked a blessing on her. They called me up to the Torah, and I named the child for my mother-in-law—may she rest in peace. The louts and loudmouths of the town who came into the bakery gave me a going over. All Frampol refreshed its spirits because of my trouble and grief. However, I resolved that I would always believe what I was told. What's the good of *not* believing? Today it's your wife you don't believe; tomorrow it's God Himself you won't take stock in.

By an apprentice who was her neighbor I sent her daily a corn or a wheat loaf, or a piece of pastry, rolls or bagels, or, when I got the chance, a slab of pudding, a slice of honeycake, or wedding strudel—whatever came my way. The apprentice was a goodhearted lad, and more than once he added something on his own. He had formerly annoyed me a lot, plucking my nose and digging me in the ribs, but when he started to be a visitor to my house he became kind and friendly. "Hey, you, Gimpel," he said to me, "you have a very decent little wife and two fine kids. You don't deserve them."

"But the things people say about her," I said.

"Well, they have long tongues," he said, "and nothing to do with them but babble. Ignore it as you ignore the cold of last winter."

One day the rabbi sent for me and said, "Are you certain, Gimpel, that you were wrong about your wife?"

I said, "I'm certain."

"Why, but look here! You yourself saw it."

"It must have been a shadow," I said.

"The shadow of what?"

"Just of one of the beams, I think."

"You can go home then. You owe thanks to the Yanover rabbi. He found an obscure reference in Maimonides that favored you."

I seized the rabbi's hand and kissed it.

I wanted to run home immediately. It's no small thing to be separated for so long a time from wife and child. Then I reflected: I'd better go back to work now, and go home in the evening. I said nothing to anyone, although as far as my heart was concerned it was like one of the Holy Days. The women teased and twitted me as they did every day, but my thought was: Go on, with your loose talk. The truth is out, like the oil upon the water. Maimonides says it's right, and therefore it is right!

At night, when I had covered the dough to let it rise, I took my share of bread and a little sack of flour and started homeward. The moon was full and the stars were glistening, something to terrify the soul. I hurried onward, and before me darted a long shadow. It was winter, and a fresh snow had fallen. I had a mind to sing, but it was growing late and I didn't want to wake the householders. Then I felt like whistling, but I remembered that you don't whistle at night because it brings the demons out. So I was silent and walked as fast as I could.

Dogs in the Christian yards barked at me when I passed, but I thought: Bark your teeth out! What are you but mere dogs? Whereas I am a man, the husband of a fine wife, the father of promising children.

As I approached the house my heart started to pound as though it were the heart of a criminal. I felt no fear, but my heart went thump! thump! Well, no drawing back. I quietly lifted the latch and went in. Elka was asleep. I looked at the infant's cradle. The shutter was closed, but the moon forced its way through the cracks.

I saw the newborn child's face and loved it as soon as I saw it—immediately—each tiny bone.

Then I came nearer to the bed. And what did I see but the apprentice lying there beside Elka. The moon went out all at once. It was utterly black, and I trembled. My teeth chattered. The bread fell from my hands, and my wife waked and said, "Who is that, ah?"

I muttered, "It's me."

"Gimpel?" she asked. "How come you're here? I thought it was forbidden."

"The rabbi said," I answered and shook as with a fever.

"Listen to me, Gimpel," she said, "go out to the shed and see if the goat's all right. It seems she's been sick." I have forgotten to say that we had a goat. When I heard she was unwell I went into the yard. The nannygoat was a good little creature. I had a nearly human feeling for her.

With hesitant steps I went up to the shed and opened the door. The goat stood there on her four feet. I felt her everywhere, drew her by the horns, examined her udders, and found nothing wrong. She had probably eaten too much bark. "Good night, little goat," I said. "Keep well." And the little beast answered with a "Maa" as though to thank me for the good will.

I went back. The apprentice had vanished.

"Where," I asked, "is the lad?"

"What lad?" my wife answered.

"What do you mean?" I said. "The apprentice. You were sleeping with him."

"The things I have dreamed this night and the night before," she said, "may they come true and lay you low, body and soul! An evil spirit has taken root in you and dazzles your sight." She screamed out, "You hateful creature! You moon calf! You spook! You uncouth man! Get out, or I'll scream all Frampol out of bed!"

Before I could move, her brother sprang out from behind the oven and struck me a blow on the back of the head. I thought he had broken my neck. I felt that something about me was deeply wrong, and I said, "Don't make a scandal. All that's needed now is that people should accuse me of raising spooks and *dybbuks*." For that was what she had meant. "No one will touch bread of my baking."

In short, I somehow calmed her.

"Well," she said, "that's enough. Lie down, and be shattered by wheels."

Next morning I called the apprentice aside. "Listen here, brother!" I said. And so on and so forth. "What do you say?" He stared at me as though I had dropped from the roof or something.

"I swear," he said, "you'd better go to an herb doctor or some healer. I'm afraid you have a screw loose, but I'll hush it up for you." And that's how the thing stood.

To make a long story short, I lived twenty years with my wife. She bore me six children, four daughters and two sons. All kinds of things happened, but I neither saw nor heard. I be-

lieved, and that's all. The rabbi recently said
to me, "Belief in itself is beneficial. It is written
that a good man lives by his faith."

Suddenly my wife took sick. It began with a
trifle, a little growth upon the breast. But she
evidently was not destined to live long; she had
no years. I spent a fortune on her. I have forgotten to say that by this time I had a bakery
of my own and in Frampol was considered to be
something of a rich man. Daily the healer came,
and every witch doctor in the neighborhood was
brought. They decided to use leeches, and after
that to try cupping. They even called a doctor
from Lublin, but it was too late. Before she died
she called me to her bed and said, "Forgive me,
Gimpel."

I said, "What is there to forgive? You have
been a good and faithful wife."

"Woe, Gimpel!" she said. "It was ugly how I
deceived you all these years. I want to go clean
to my Maker, and so I have to tell you that the
children are not yours."

If I had been clouted on the head with a piece
of wood it couldn't have bewildered me more.

"Whose are they?" I asked.

"I don't know," she said. "There were a
lot ... but they're not yours." And as she spoke
she tossed her head to the side, her eyes turned
glassy, and it was all up with Elka. On her
whitened lips there remained a smile.

I imagined that, dead as she was, she was
saying, "I deceived Gimpel. That was the meaning of my brief life."

IV

One night, when the period of mourning was done, as I lay dreaming on the flour sacks, there came the Spirit of Evil himself and said to me, "Gimpel, why do you sleep?"

I said, "What should I be doing? Eating *kreplach?*"

"The whole world deceives you," he said, "and you ought to deceive the world in your turn."

"How can I deceive all the world?" I asked him.

He answered, "You might accumulate a bucket of urine every day and at night pour it into the dough. Let the sages of Frampol eat filth."

"What about the judgment in the world to come?" I said.

"There is no world to come," he said. "They've sold you a bill of goods and talked you into believing you carried a cat in your belly. What nonsense!"

"Well then," I said, "and is there a God?"

He answered, "There is no God either."

"What," I said, *"is* there, then?"

"A thick mire."

He stood before my eyes with a goatish beard and horn, long-toothed, and with a tail. Hearing such words, I wanted to snatch him by the tail, but I tumbled from the flour sacks and nearly broke a rib. Then it happened that I had to answer the call of nature, and, passing, I saw the risen dough, which seemed to say to me, "Do it!" In brief, I let myself be persuaded.

At dawn the apprentice came. We kneaded the bread, scattered caraway seeds on it, and set it to bake. Then the apprentice went away, and I was left sitting in the little trench by the oven, on a pile of rags. Well, Gimpel, I thought, you've revenged yourself on them for all the shame they've put on you. Outside the frost glittered, but it was warm beside the oven. The flames heated my face. I bent my head and fell into a doze.

I saw in a dream, at once, Elka in her shroud. She called to me, "What have you done, Gimpel?"

I said to her, "It's all your fault," and started to cry.

"You fool!" she said. "You fool! Because I was false is everything false too? I never deceived anyone but myself. I'm paying for it all, Gimpel. They spare you nothing here."

I looked at her face. It was black; I was startled and waked, and remained sitting dumb. I sensed that everything hung in the balance. A false step now and I'd lose Eternal Life. But God gave me His help. I seized the long shovel and took out the loaves, carried them into the yard, and started to dig a hole in the frozen earth.

My apprentice came back as I was doing it. "What are you doing, boss?" he said, and grew pale as a corpse.

"I know what I'm doing," I said, and I buried it all before his very eyes.

Then I went home, took my hoard from its hiding place, and divided it among the children. "I saw your mother tonight," I said. "She's turning black, poor thing."

They were so astounded they couldn't speak a word.

"Be well," I said, "and forget that such a one as Gimpel ever existed." I put on my short coat, a pair of boots, took the bag that held my prayer shawl in one hand, my stock in the other, and kissed the *mezzuzah*. When people saw me in the street they were greatly surprised.

"Where are you going?" they said.

I answered, "Into the world." And so I departed from Frampol.

I wandered over the land, and good people did not neglect me. After many years I became old and white; I heard a great deal, many lies and falsehoods, but the longer I lived the more I understood that there were really no lies. Whatever doesn't really happen is dreamed at night. It happens to one if it doesn't happen to another, tomorrow if not today, or a century hence if not next year. What difference can it make? Often I heard tales of which I said, "Now this is a thing that cannot happen." But before a year had elapsed I heard that it actually had come to pass somewhere.

Going from place to place, eating at strange tables, it often happens that I spin yarns—im-

probable things that could never have happened—about devils, magicians, windmills, and
the like. The children run after me, calling,
"Grandfather, tell us a story." Sometimes they
ask for particular stories, and I try to please
them. A fat young boy once said to me, "Grandfather, it's the same story you told us before."
The little rogue, he was right.

So it is with dreams too. It is many years
since I left Frampol, but as soon as I shut my
eyes I am there again. And whom do you think
I see? Elka. She is standing by the washtub, as
at our first encounter, but her face is shining
and her eyes are as radiant as the eyes of a
saint, and she speaks outlandish words to me,
strange things. When I wake I have forgotten
it all. But while the dream lasts I am comforted.
She answers all my queries, and what comes
out is that all is right. I weep and implore, "Let
me be with you." And she consoles me and tells
me to be patient. The time is nearer than it is
far. Sometimes she strokes and kisses me and
weeps upon my face. When I awaken I feel her
lips and taste the salt of her tears.

No doubt the world is entirely an imaginary
world, but it is only once removed from the true
world. At the door of the hovel where I lie, there
stands the plank on which the dead are taken
away. The gravedigger Jew has his spade ready.
The grave waits and the worms are hungry; the
shrouds are prepared—I carry them in my beggar's sack. Another *shnorrer* is waiting to in-

herit my bed of straw. When the time comes I will go joyfully. Whatever may be there, it will be real, without complication, without ridicule, without deception. God be praised: there even Gimpel cannot be deceived.

Translated by Saul Bellow

THE GENTLEMAN
FROM CRACOW

I

Amid thick forests and deep swamps, on the slope of a hill, level at the summit, lay the village of Frampol. Nobody knew who had founded it, or why just there. Goats grazed among the tombstones which were already sunk in the ground of the cemetery. In the community house there was a parchment with a chronicle on it, but the first page was missing and the writing had faded. Legends were current among the people, tales of wicked intrigue concerning a mad nobleman, a lascivious lady, a Jewish scholar, and a wild dog. But their true origin was lost in the past.

Peasants who tilled the surrounding countryside were poor; the land was stubborn. In the village, the Jews were impoverished; their roofs were straw, their floors dirt. In summer many of them wore no shoes, and in cold weather they wrapped their feet in rags or wore sandals made of straw.

Rabbi Ozer, although renowned for his erudition, received a salary of only eighteen *groszy* a week. The assistant rabbi, besides being ritual slaughterer, was teacher, matchmaker,

bath attendant, and poorhouse nurse as well.
Even those villagers who were considered
wealthy knew little of luxury. They wore cotton
gabardines, tied about their waists with string,
and tasted meat only on the Sabbath. Gold coin
was rarely seen in Frampol.

But the inhabitants of Frampol had been
blessed with fine children. The boys grew tall
and strong, the girls handsome. It was a mixed
blessing, however, for the young men left to
marry girls from other towns, while their sisters, who had no dowries, remained unwed. Yet
despite everything, inexplicably, though the
food was scarce and the water foul, the children
continued to thrive.

Then, one summer, there was a drought.
Even the oldest peasants could not recall a calamity such as this one. No rain fell. The corn
was parched and stunted. There was scarcely
anything worth harvesting. Not until the few
sheaves of wheat had been cut and gathered did
the rain come, and with it hail which destroyed
whatever grain the drought had spared. Locusts
huge as birds came in the wake of the storm;
human voices were said to issue from their
throats. They flew at the eyes of the peasants
who tried to drive them away. That year there
was no fair, for everything had been lost. Neither the peasants nor the Jews of Frampol had
food. Although there was grain in the large
towns, no one could buy it.

Just when all hope had been abandoned and

the entire town was about to go begging, a miracle occurred. A carriage drawn by eight spirited horses, came into Frampol. The villagers expected its occupant to be a Christian gentleman, but it was a Jew, a young man between the ages of twenty and thirty, who alighted. Tall and pale, with a round black beard and fiery dark eyes, he wore a sable hat, silver-buckled shoes, and a beaver-trimmed caftan. Around his waist was a green silk sash. Aroused, the entire town rushed to get a glimpse of the stranger. This is the story he told: He was a doctor, a widower from Cracow. His wife, the daughter of a wealthy merchant, had died with their baby in childbirth.

Overwhelmed, the villagers asked why he had come to Frampol. It was on the advice of a Wonder Rabbi, he told them. The melancholy he had known after his wife's death, would, the rabbi assured him, disappear in Frampol. From the poorhouse the beggars came, crowding about him as he distributed alms—three groszy, six groszy, half-gulden pieces. The stranger was clearly a gift from Heaven, and Frampol was not destined to vanish. The beggars hurried to the baker for bread, and the baker sent to Zamosc for a sack of flour.

"One sack?" the young doctor asked. "Why that won't last a single day. I will order a wagonload, and not only flour, but cornmeal also."

"But we have no money," the village elders explained.

"God willing, you will repay me when times are good," and saying this, the stranger produced a purse crammed with golden ducats. Frampol rejoiced as he counted out the coins.

The next day, wagons filled with flour, buckwheat, barley, millet, and beans, drove into Frampol. News of the village's good fortune reached the ears of the peasants, and they came to the Jews, to buy goods, as the Egyptians had once come to Joseph. Being without money, they paid in kind; as a result, there was meat in town. Now the ovens burned once more; the pots were full. Smoke rose from the chimneys, sending the odors of roast chicken and goose, onion and garlic, fresh bread and pastry, into the evening air. The villagers returned to their occupations; shoemakers mended shoes; tailors picked up their rusted shears and irons.

The evenings were warm and the sky clear, though the Feast of the Tabernacles had already passed. The stars seemed unusually large. Even the birds were awake, and they chirped and warbled as though in mid-summer. The stranger from Cracow had taken the best room at the inn, and his dinner consisted of broiled duck, marchpane, and twisted bread. Apricots and Hungarian wine were his dessert. Six candles adorned the table. One evening after dinner, the doctor from Cracow entered the large public room where some of the more inquisitive townspeople had gathered and asked,

"Would anyone care for a game of cards?"

"But it isn't Chanukah yet," they answered in surprise.

"Why wait for Chanukah? I'll put up a gulden for every groszy."

A few of the more frivolous men were willing to try their luck, and it turned out to be good. A groszy meant a gulden, and one gulden became thirty. Anyone played who wished to do so. Everybody won. But the stranger did not seem distressed. Banknotes and coins of silver and gold covered the table. Women and girls crowded into the room, and it seemed as though the gleam of the gold before them was reflected in their eyes. They gasped in wonderment. Never before in Frampol had such things happened. Mothers cautioned their daughters to take pains with their hair, and allowed them to dress in holiday clothes. The girl who found favor in the eyes of the young doctor would be fortunate; he was not one to require a dowry.

II

The next morning, matchmakers called on him, each extolling the virtues of the girl he represented. The doctor invited them to be seated, served them honey cake, macaroons, nuts, and mead, and announced:

"From each of you I get exactly the same story: Your client is beautiful and clever and possesses every possible distinction. But how can I know which of you is telling the truth? I want the finest of them all as my wife. Here is what I suggest: Let there be a ball to which all the eligible young women are invited. By observing their appearance and behavior, I shall be able to choose among them. Then the marriage contract will be drawn and the wedding arranged."

The matchmakers were astounded. Old Mendel was the first to find words. "A ball? That sort of thing is all right for rich Gentiles, but we Jews have not indulged in such festivities since the destruction of the Temple—except when the Law prescribes it for certain holidays."

"Isn't every Jew obliged to marry off his daughters?" asked the doctor.

"But the girls have no appropriate clothes," another matchmaker protested. "Because of the drought they would have to go in rags."

"I will see that they all have clothes. I'll order enough silk, wool, velvet, and linen from Zamosc to outfit every girl. Let the ball take place. Let it be one that Frampol will never forget."

"But where can we hold it?" another matchmaker interjected. "The hall where we used to hold weddings has burned down, and our cottages are too small."

"There's the market place," the gentleman from Cracow suggested.

"But it is already the month of Heshvan. Any day now, it will turn cold."

"We'll choose a warm night when the moon is out. Don't worry about it."

To all the numerous objections of the matchmakers, the stranger had an answer ready. Finally they agreed to consult the elders. The doctor said he was in no hurry, he would await their decision. During the entire discussion, he had been carrying on a game of chess with one of the town's cleverest young men, while munching raisins.

The elders were incredulous when they heard what had been proposed. But the young girls were excited. The young men approved also. The mothers pretended to hesitate, but finally gave their consent. When a delegation of the older men sought out Rabbi Ozer for his approval, he was outraged.

"What kind of charlatan is this?" he shouted. "Frampol is not Cracow. All we need is a ball! Heaven forbid that we bring down a plague, and innocent infants be made to pay for our frivolity!"

But the more practical of the men reasoned with the rabbi, saying, "Our daughters walk around barefoot and in tatters now. He will provide them with shoes and clothing. If one of them should please him he would marry her and settle here. Certainly that is to our advantage. The synagogue needs a new roof. The windowpanes of the house of study are broken, the bathhouse is badly in need of repairs. In the poorhouse the sick lie on bundles of rotting straw."

"All this is true. But suppose we sin?"

"Everything will be done according to the Law, Rabbi. You can trust us."

Taking down the book of the Law, Rabbi Ozer leafed through it. Occasionally he stopped to study a page, and then, finally, after sighing and hesitating, he consented. Was there any choice? He himself had received no salary for six months.

As soon as the rabbi had given his consent there was a great display of activity. The dry goods merchants traveled immediately to Zamosc and Yanev, returning with cloth and leather paid for by the gentleman from Cracow. The tailors and seamstresses worked day and night; the cobblers left their benches only to pray. The young women, all anticipation, were in a feverish state. Vaguely remembered dance steps were tried out. They baked cakes and other pastries, and used up their stores of jams and preserves which they had been keeping in readiness for illness. The Frampol musicians were equally active. Cymbals, fiddles, and bagpipes, long forgotten and neglected, had to be dusted off and tuned. Gaiety infected even the very old, for it was rumored that the elegant doctor planned a banquet for the poor where alms would be distributed.

The eligible girls were wholly concerned with self-improvement. They scrubbed their skin and arranged their hair; a few even visited the ritual bath to bathe among the married women.

In the evenings, faces flushed, eyes sparkling, they met at each other's houses, to tell stories and ask riddles. It was difficult for them, and for their mothers as well, to sleep at night. Fathers sighed as they slept. And suddenly the young girls of Frampol seemed so attractive that the young men who had contemplated marrying outside of town fell in love with them. Although the young men still sat in the study-house poring over the Talmud, its wisdom no longer penetrated to them. It was the ball alone that they spoke of now, only the ball that occupied their thoughts.

The doctor from Cracow also enjoyed himself. He changed his clothes several times daily. First it was a silk coat worn with pom-pommed slippers, then a woolen caftan with high boots. At one meal he wore a pelerine trimmed with beaver tails, and at the next a cape embroidered with flowers and leaves. He breakfasted on roast pigeon which he washed down with dry wine. For lunch he ordered egg noodles and blintzes, and he was audacious enough to eat Sabbath pudding on weekdays. He never attended prayer, but instead played all sorts of games: cards, goats and wolves, coin-pitching. Having finished lunch, he would drive through the neighborhood with his coachman. The peasants would lift their hats as he passed, and bow almost to the ground. One day he strolled through Frampol with a gold-headed cane. Women crowded to the windows to observe him, and boys, following after him, picked up the rock candy he tossed them. In the evenings he and his companions, gay young men, drank wine until all hours. Rabbi Ozer constantly warned his flock that they walked a downhill path led by the Evil One, but they paid no attention to him. Their minds and hearts were completely possessed by the ball, which would be held at the market place in the middle of that month, at the time of the full moon.

III

At the edge of town, in a small valley close to a swamp, stood a hut no larger than a chicken coop. Its floor was dirt, its window was boarded; and the roof, because it was covered with green and yellow moss, made one think of a bird's nest that had been forsaken. Heaps of garbage were strewn before the hut, and lime ditches furrowed the soggy earth. Amidst the refuse there was an occasional chair without a seat, a jug missing an ear, a table without legs. Every type of broom, bone, and rag seemed to be rotting there. This was where Lipa the Ragpicker lived with his daughter, Hodle. While his first wife was alive, Lipa had been a respected merchant in Frampol where he occupied a pew at the east wall of the synagogue. But after his wife had drowned herself in the river, his condition declined rapidly. He took to drink, associated with the town's worst element, and soon ended up bankrupt.

His second wife, a beggar woman from Yanev, bore him a daughter whom she left behind when she deserted him for non-support. Unconcerned about his wife's departure, Lipa allowed the child to shift for herself. Each week he spent a few days collecting rags from the garbage. The rest of the time he was in the tavern. Although the innkeeper's wife scolded him, she received only abusive answers in reply. Lipa had his success among the men as a tale-spinner. He attracted business to the place with his fantastic yarns about witches and windmills and devils and goblins. He could also recite Polish and Ukrainian rhymes and had a knack for telling jokes. The innkeeper allowed him to occupy a place near the stove, and from time to time he was given a bowl of soup and a piece of bread. Old friends, remembering Lipa's former affluence, occasionally presented him with a pair of pants, a threadbare coat, or a shirt. He accepted everything ungraciously. He even stuck out his tongue at his benefactors as they turned away from him.

As in the saying, "Like father, like son," Hodle inherited the vices of both parents—her drunken father, her begging mother. By the time she was six, she had won a reputation as a glutton and thief. Barefoot and half naked, she roamed the town, entering houses and raiding the larders of those who were not home. She preyed on chickens and ducks, cut their throats with glass, and ate them. Although the inhabitants of Frampol had often warned her father that he was rearing a wanton, the information did not seem to bother him. He seldom spoke to her and she did not even call him father. When she was twelve, her lasciviousness became a matter for discussion among the women. Gypsies visited her shack, and it was rumored that she devoured the meat of cats and dogs, in fact, every kind of carcass. Tall and lean, with red hair and green eyes, she went barefoot summer and winter, and her skirts were made of colored scraps discarded by the seamstresses. She was feared by mothers who said she wove spells that blighted the young. The village elders who admonished her received brazen answers. She had the shrewdness of a bastard, the quick tongue of an adder, and when attacked by street urchins, did not hesitate to strike back. Particularly skilled in swearing, she had an unlimited repertoire. It was like her to call out, "Pox on your tongue and gangrene in your eyes," or, possibly, "May you rot till the skunks run from your smell."

Occasionally her curses were effective, and the town grew wary of incurring her anger. But as she matured she tended to avoid the town proper, and the time came when she was almost forgotten. But on the day that the Frampol merchants, in preparation for the ball, distributed cloth and leather among the town's young women, Hodle reappeared. She was now about seventeen, fully grown, though still in short skirts; her face was freckled, and her hair disheveled. Beads, such as those worn by gypsies, encircled her throat, and on her wrists were bracelets made from wolves' teeth. Pushing her way through the crowd, she demanded her share. There was nothing left but a few odds and ends, which were given to her. Furious with her allotment, she hastened home with it. Those who had seen what had happened laughed, "Look who's going to the ball! What a pretty picture she'll make!"

At last the shoemakers and tailors were done; every dress fit, every shoe was right. The days were miraculously warm, and the nights as luminous as the evenings of Pentecost. It was the morning star that, on the day of the ball, woke the entire town. Tables and benches lined one side of the market. The cooks had already roasted calves, sheep, goats, geese, ducks, and chicken, and had baked sponge and raisin cakes, braided bread and rolls, onion biscuits and ginger bread. There were mead and beer and a barrel of Hungarian wine that had been brought by the wine dealer. When the children arrived they brought the bows and arrows with which they were accustomed to play at the Omer feast, as well as their Purim rattles and Torah flags. Even the doctor's horses were decorated with willow branches and autumn flowers, and the coachman paraded them through the town. Apprentices left their work, and yeshiva students their volumes of the Talmud. And despite Rabbi Ozer's injunction against the young matrons' attending the ball, they dressed in their wedding gowns and went, arriving with the young girls, who also came in white, each bearing a candle in her hand as though she were a bridesmaid. The band had already begun to play, and the music was lively. Rabbi Ozer alone was not present, having locked himself in his study. His maidservant had gone to the ball, leaving him to himself. He knew no good could come of such behavior, but there was nothing he could do to prevent it.

By late afternoon all the girls had gathered in the market place, surrounded by the townspeople. Drums were beaten. Jesters performed. The girls danced; first a quadrille, then a scissor dance. Next it was Kozack, and finally the Dance of Anger. Now the moon appeared, although the sun had not yet set. It was time for the gentleman from Cracow. He entered on a white mare, flanked by bodyguards and his best man. He wore a large-plumed hat, and silver buttons flashed on his green coat. A sword hung at his side, and his shiny boots rested in the stirrups. He resembled a gentleman off to war with his entourage. Silently he sat in his saddle, watching the girls as they danced. How graceful they were, how charmingly they moved! But one who did not dance was the daughter of Lipa the Ragpicker. She stood to one side, ignored by them all.

IV

The setting sun, remarkably large, stared down angrily like a heavenly eye upon the Frampol market place. Never before had Frampol seen such a sunset. Like rivers of burning sulphur, fiery clouds streamed across the heavens, assuming the shapes of elephants, lions, snakes, and monsters. They seemed to be waging a battle in the sky, devouring one another, spitting, breathing fire. It almost seemed to be the River of Fire they watched, where demons tortured the evil-doers amidst glowing coals and heaps of ashes. The moon swelled, became vast, blood-red, spotted, scarred, and gave off little light. The evening grew very dark, dissolving even the stars. The young men fetched torches, and a barrel of burning pitch was prepared. Shadows danced back and forth as though attending a ball of their own. Around the market place the houses seemed to vibrate; roofs quivered, chimneys shook. Such gaiety and intoxication had never before been known in Frampol. Everyone, for the first time in months, had eaten and drunk sufficiently. Even the animals participated in the merrymaking. Horses neighed, cows mooed, and the few roosters that had survived the slaughter of the fowl crowed. Flocks of crows and strange birds flew in to pick at the leavings. Fireflies illumined the darkness, and lightning flashed on the horizon. But there was no thunder. A weird circular light glowed in the sky for a few moments and then suddenly plummeted toward the horizon, a crimson tail behind it, resembling a burning rod. Then, as everyone stared in wonder at the sky, the gentleman from Cracow spoke:

"Listen to me. I have wonderful things to tell you, but let no one be overcome by joy. Men, take hold of your wives. Young men, look to your girls. You see in me the wealthiest man in the entire world. Money is sand to me, and diamonds are pebbles. I come from the land of Ophir, where King Solomon found the gold for his temple. I dwell in the palace of the Queen of Sheba. My coach is solid gold, its wheels inlaid with sapphires, with axles of ivory, its lamps studded with rubies and emeralds, opals and amethysts. The Ruler of the Ten Lost Tribes of Israel knows of your miseries, and he has sent me to be your benefactor. But there is one condition. Tonight, every virgin must marry. I will provide a dowry of ten thousand ducats for each maiden, as well as a string of pearls that will hang to her knees. But make haste. Every girl must have a husband before the clocks strike twelve."

The crowd was hushed. It was as quiet as New Year's Day before the blowing of the ram's horn. One could hear the buzzing of a fly.

Then one old man called out, "But that's impossible. The girls are not even engaged!"

"Let them become engaged."

"To whom?"

"We can draw lots," the gentleman from Cracow replied. "Whoever is to be married will have his or her name written on a card. Mine also. And then we shall draw to see who is meant for whom."

"But a girl must wait seven days. She must have the prescribed ablutions."

"Let the sin be on me. She needn't wait."

Despite the protestations of the old men and their wives, a sheet of paper was torn into pieces, and on each piece the name of a young man or young woman was written by a scribe. The town's beadle, now in the service of the gentleman from Cracow, drew from one skullcap the names of the young men, and from another those of the young women, chanting their names to the same tune with which he called up members of the congregation for the reading of the Torah.

"Nahum, son of Katriel, betrothed to Yentel, daughter of Nathan. Solomon, son of Cov Baer, betrothed to Tryna, daughter of Jonah Lieb." The assortment was a strange one, but since in the night all sheep are black, the matches seemed reasonable enough. After each drawing, the newly engaged couple, hand in hand, approached the doctor to collect the dowry and wedding gift. As he had promised, the gentleman from Cracow gave each the stipulated sum of ducats, and on the neck of each bride he hung a strand of pearls. Now the mothers, unable to

restrain their joy, began to dance and shout.
The fathers stood by, bewildered. When the
girls lifted their dresses to catch the gold coins
given by the doctor, their legs and underclothing were exposed, which sent the men into paroxysms of lust. Fiddles screeched, drums
pounded, trumpets blared. The uproar was deafening. Twelve-year-old boys were mated with
"spinsters" of nineteen. The sons of substantial
citizens took the daughters of paupers as brides;
midgets were coupled with giants, beauties
with cripples. On the last two slips appeared
the names of the gentleman from Cracow and
Hodle, the daughter of Lipa the Ragpicker.

The same old man who had called out previously said, "Woe unto us, the girl is a harlot."

"Come to me, Hodle, come to your bridegroom," the doctor bade.

Hodle, her hair in two long braids, dressed
in a calico skirt, and with sandals on her feet,
did not wait to be asked twice. As soon as she
had been called she walked to where the gentleman from Cracow sat on his mare, and fell to
her knees. She prostrated herself seven times
before him.

"Is it true, what that old fool says?" her prospective husband asked her.

"Yes, my lord, it is so."

"Have you sinned only with Jews or with
Gentiles as well?"

"With both."

"Was it for bread?"

"No. For the sheer pleasure."

"How old were you when you started?"

"Not quite ten."

"Are you sorry for what you have done?"

"No."

"Why not?"

"Why should I be?" she answered shamelessly.

"You don't fear the tortures of hell?"

"I fear nothing—not even God. There is no God."

Once more the old man began to scream, "Woe to us, woe to us, Jews! A fire is upon us, burning, Jews, Satan's fire. Save your souls, Jews. Flee, before it is too late!"

"Gag him," the gentleman from Cracow commanded.

The guards seized the old man and gagged him. The doctor, leading Hodle by the hand, began to dance. Now, as though the powers of darkness had been summoned, the rain and hail began to fall; flashes of lightning were accompanied by mighty thunderclaps. But, heedless of the storm, pious men and women embraced without shame, dancing and shouting as though possessed. Even the old were affected. In the furor, dresses were ripped, shoes shaken off, hats, wigs and skullcaps trampled in the mud. Sashes, slipping to the ground, twisted there like snakes. Suddenly there was a terrific crash. A huge bolt of lightning had simultaneously struck the synagogue, the study house, and the ritual bath. The whole town was on fire.

Now at last the deluded people realized that

there was no natural origin to these occur-
rences. Although the rain continued to fall and
even increased in intensity, the fire was not
extinguished. An eerie light glowed in the market place. Those few prudent individuals who
tried to disengage themselves from the demented crowd were crushed to earth and trampled.

And then the gentleman from Cracow revealed his true identity. He was no longer the
young man the villagers had welcomed, but a
creature covered with scales, with an eye in his
chest, and on his forehead a horn that rotated
at great speed. His arms were covered with hair,
thorns, and elflocks, and his tail was a mass of
live serpents, for he was none other than Ketev
Mriri, Chief of the Devils.

Witches, werewolves, imps, demons, and
hobgoblins plummeted from the sky, some on
brooms, others on hoops, still others on spiders.
Osnath, the daughter of Machlath, her fiery
hair loosened in the wind, her breasts bare and
thighs exposed, leaped from chimney to chimney, and skated along the eaves. Namah, Hur-
mizah the daughter of Aff, and many other she-
devils did all sorts of somersaults. Satan himself gave away the bridegroom, while four evil
spirits held the poles of the canopy, which had
turned into writhing pythons. Four dogs escorted the groom. Hodle's dress fell from her
and she stood naked. Her breasts hung down to
her navel and her feet were webbed. Her hair

was a wilderness of worms and caterpillars. The groom held out a triangular ring and, instead of saying, "With this ring be thou consecrated to me according to the laws of Moses and Israel," he said, "With this ring, be thou desecrated to me according to the blasphemy of Korah and Ishmael." And instead of wishing the pair good luck, the evil spirits called out, "Bad luck," and they began to chant:

"The curse of Eve, the Mark of Cain,
The cunning of the snake, unite the twain."

Screaming for the last time, the old man clutched at his head and died. Ketev Mriri began his eulogy:

"Devil's dung and Satan's spell
Bring his ghost to roast in hell."

V

In the middle of the night, old Rabbi Ozer awoke. Since he was a holy man, the fire which was consuming the town had no power over his house. Sitting up in bed he looked about, wondering if dawn were already breaking. But it was neither day nor night without. The sky was a fiery red, and from the distance came a clamor of shouts and songs that resembled the howling of wild beasts. At first, recalling nothing, the old man wondered what was going on. "Has the world come to an end? Or have I failed to hear the ram's horn heralding the Messiah? Has He arrived?" Washing his hands, he put on his slippers and overcoat and went out.

The town was unrecognizable. Where houses had been, only chimneys stood. Mounds of coal smoldered here and there. He called the beadle, but there was no answer. With his cane, the rabbi went searching for his flock.

"Where are you, Jews, where are you?" he called piteously.

The earth scorched his feet, but he did not slacken his pace. Mad dogs and strange beings attacked him, but he wielded his cane against them. His sorrow was so great that he felt no fear. Where the market place used to be, a terrible sight met him. There was nothing but one great swamp, full of mud, slime, and ashes. Floundering in mud up to their waists, a crowd of naked people went through the movements of dance. At first, the rabbi mistook the weirdly moving figures for devils, and was about to recite the chapter, "Let there be contentment," and other passages dealing with exorcism, when he recognized the men of his town. Only then did he remember the doctor from Cracow, and the rabbi cried out bitterly, "Jews, for the sake of God, save your souls! You are in the hands of Satan!"

But the townspeople, too entranced to heed

his cries, continued their frenzied movements for a long time, jumping like frogs, shaking as though with fever. With hair uncovered and breasts bare, the women laughed, cried, and swayed. Catching a yeshiva boy by his side-locks, a girl pulled him to her lap. A woman tugged at the beard of a strange man. Old men and women were immersed in slime up to their loins. They scarcely looked alive.

Relentlessly, the rabbi urged the people to resist evil. Reciting the Torah and other holy books, as well as incantations and the several names of God, he succeeded in rousing some of them. Soon others responded. The rabbi had helped the first man from the mire, then that one assisted the next, and so on. Most of them had recovered by the time the morning star appeared. Perhaps the spirits of their forbears had interceded, for although many had sinned, only one man had died this night in the market place square.

Now the men were appalled, realizing that the devil had bewitched them, had dragged them through muck; and they wept.

"Where is our money?" the girls wailed, "And our gold and our jewelry? Where is our clothing? What happened to the wine, the mead, the wedding gifts?"

But everything had turned to mud; the town of Frampol, stripped and ruined, had become a swamp. Its inhabitants were mud-splashed, denuded, monstrous. For a moment, forgetting their grief, they laughed at each other. The hair of the girls had turned into elflocks, and bats were entangled there. The young men had grown gray and wrinkled; the old were yellow as corpses. In their midst lay the old man who had died. Crimson with shame, the sun rose.

"Let us rend our clothes in mourning," one man called, but his words evoked laughter, for all were naked.

"We are doomed, my sisters," lamented a woman.

"Let us drown ourselves in the river," a girl shrieked. "Why go on living?"

One of the yeshiva boys said, "Let us strangle ourselves with our sashes."

"Brothers, we are lost. Let us blaspheme God," said a horse dealer.

"Have you lost your minds, Jews?" cried Rabbi Ozer, "Repent, before it is too late. You have fallen into Satan's snare, but it is my fault, I take the sin upon myself. I am the guilty one. I will be your scapegoat, and you shall remain clean."

"This is madness!" one of the scholars protested, "God forbid that there be so many sins on your holy head!"

"Do not worry about that. My shoulders are broad. I should have had more foresight. I was blind not to realize that the Cracow doctor was the Evil One. And when the shepherd is blind, the flock goes astray. It is I who deserve the punishment, the curses."

"Rabbi, what shall we do? We have no homes, no bed clothes, nothing. Woe to us, to our bodies and to our souls."

"Our babies!" cried the young matrons, "Let us hurry to them!"

But it was the infants who had been the real victims of the passion for gold that had caused the inhabitants of Frampol to transgress. The infants' cribs were burned, their little bones were charred. The mothers stooped to pick up little hands, feet, skulls. The wailing and crying lasted long, but how long can a whole town weep? The gravedigger gathered the bones and carried them to the cemetery. Half the town began the prescribed seven days of mourning. But all fasted, for there was no food anywhere.

But the compassion of the Jews is well known, and when the neighboring town of Yanev learned what had happened, clothing, bed linen, bread, cheese, and dishes were collected and sent to Frampol. Timber merchants brought logs for building. A rich man offered credit. The next day the reconstruction of the town was begun. Although work is forbidden to those in mourning, Rabbi Ozer issued a verdict that this was an exceptional case: the lives of the people were in danger. Miraculously, the weather remained mild; no snow fell. Never before had there been such diligence in Frampol. The inhabitants built and prayed, mixed lime with sand, and recited psalms. The women worked with the men, while girls, forgetting their fastidiousness, helped also. Scholars and men of high position assisted. Peasants from the surrounding villages, hearing of the catastrophe, took the old and infirm into their homes. They also brought wood, potatoes, cabbages, onions and other food. Priests and bishops from Lublin, hearing of events that suggested witchcraft, came to examine witnesses. As the scribe recorded the names of those living in Frampol, Hodle, the daughter of Lipa the Ragpicker, was suddenly remembered. But when the townspeople went to where her hut had been, they found the hill covered with weeds and bramble, silent save for the cries of crows and cats; there was no indication that human beings had ever dwelt there.

Then it was understood that Hodle was in truth Lilith, and that the host of the netherworld had come to Frampol because of her. After their investigations, the clergymen from Lublin, greatly astonished at what they had seen and heard, returned home. A few days later, the day before the Sabbath, Rabbi Ozer died. The entire town attended his funeral, and the town preacher said a eulogy for him.

In time, a new rabbi came to the community, and a new town arose. The old people died, the mounds in the cemetery sifted down, and the monuments slowly sank. But the story, signed by trustworthy witnesses, can still be read in the parchment chronicle.

And the events in the story brought their

epilogue: the lust for gold had been stifled in Frampol; it was never rekindled. From generation to generation the people remained paupers. A gold coin became an abomination in Frampol, and even silver was looked at askance. Whenever a shoemaker or tailor asked too high a price for his work he was told, "Go to the gentleman from Cracow and he will give you buckets of gold."

And on the grave of Rabbi Ozer, in the memorial chapel, there burns an eternal light. A white pigeon is often seen on the roof: the sainted spirit of Rabbi Ozer.

Translated by Martha Glicklich
and Elaine Gottlieb

THE WIFE KILLER

A Folk Tale

I

I am from Turbin, and there we had a wife killer. Pelte was his name, Pelte the Wife Killer. He had four wives and, may it not be held against him, he sent them all off to the other side. What women saw in him, I don't know. He was a little man, thickset, gray, with a scraggly beard and bulging bloodshot eyes. Merely to look at him was frightful. And as for his stinginess—you never saw anything like it. Summer and winter he went about in the same padded caftan and rawhide boots. Yet he was rich. He had a sizeable brick house, a storeroom full of grain, and property in town. He had an oak chest which I remember to this day. It was covered with leather and bound with copper hoops, for protection in case of fire. To keep it safe from thieves, he had it nailed to the floor. It was said that he kept a fortune in it. All the same, I cannot understand how a woman could go to the bridal canopy with such a man. The first two wives at least had the excuse that they came from poor homes. The first one—poor soul may you live long—was an orphan, and he took her just as she was, without any dowry. The second one, on the other hand—may she rest in peace—was a widow without a cent to her name. She didn't have even an undershirt, if you'll pardon the expression. Today people talk of love. They think that once upon a time men were angels. Nonsense. Clumsy creature that he was, he fell head over heels in love with her, so that all Turbin snickered. He was already a man in his forties and she was a mere child, eighteen years or even less. In short, kind souls intervened, relatives took a hand in the matter, and things came to a head.

Right after the wedding the young wife began to complain that he wasn't acting right. Strange tales were told—may God not punish me for my words. He was spiteful all the time. Before he went to pray in the morning, she would ask him, "What do you want for lunch? Soup or borscht?" "Soup," he might say. So she'd make him soup. He'd return later and complain, "Didn't I tell you to make borscht?" She'd argue, "You said yourself that you wanted soup." And he would say, "So now I am a liar!" And before you could turn around he was already in a rage, and would grab a slice of bread and a head of garlic, and run back to the synagogue to eat there. She would run after him and shout, "I'll cook you a borscht! Don't shame me before people!" But he wouldn't even look back. In the synagogue young men sat studying. "What happened that you eat here?" they would ask him. "My wife chased me out," he would say. To make a long story short, he drove her to the grave with his tantrums. When people advised her to divorce him, he threatened to run off and abandon her. Once he did run away and was caught on the Yanov road, near the turnpike. The woman saw that she was lost, so she simply lay down in bed and died. "I am dying because of him," she said. "May it not be held against him." The entire town was aroused. Some butchers and young bloods wanted to teach him a lesson, because she was of their class, but the community would not allow it—after all, he was a well-to-do man. The dead are buried, as people say, and what the earth swallows is soon forgotten.

Some years passed and he didn't remarry. Perhaps he didn't want to, perhaps there was no suitable opportunity; anyway, he remained a widower. Women gloated over this. He became even stingier than before, and so unkempt that it was positively disgusting. He ate a bit of meat only on Saturday: scraps or derma. All week he ate dry food. He baked his own bread of corn and bran. He didn't buy wood. Instead, he went out at night with a sack, to pick up the chips near the bakery. He had two deep pockets and whatever he saw, he put into them: bones, bark, string, shards. He hid all these in his attic. He piled heaps of stuff as high as the roof. "Every little thing comes in handy," he used to say. He was a scholar in the bargain, and could quote Scripture on every occasion, though as a rule he talked little.

Everybody thought he would remain alone the rest of his life. Suddenly the terrible news spread that he was engaged to Reb Falik's Finkl. How should I describe Finkl to you! She was the most beautiful woman in town, and of the very best family. Her father, Reb Falik, was a magnate. It was said that he bound his books in silk. Whenever a bride was led to the *mikveh,* the musicians would stop before his windows and play a tune. Finkl was his only child. There had been seven and she alone survived. Reb Falik married her off to a rich young man from Brod, one in a million, learned and wise, a real aristocrat. I saw him only once as he went by, with curly *peios* and a flowered caftan and fine shoes and white socks. Blood and milk. But it was fated otherwise. Right after the Seven Blessings he collapsed. Zishe the Healer was called, and he put leeches on him and bled him, but what can you do against fate? Reb Falik rushed a carriage to Lublin to bring a doctor, but Lublin is far, and before you knew it, it was all over with him. The entire town wept, as on Yom Kippur at Kol Nidre. The old rabbi—may he rest in peace—delivered the eulogy. I am only a sinful woman and I don't know much of learned matters, but I remember to this day what the rabbi said. Everybody memorized the eulogy. "He ordered black and got white . . ." the rabbi began. In the Gemorra this is about a man ordering pigeons, but the rabbi—peace be on him—made it mean wedding garments and burial shrouds. Even enemies mourned. We girls soaked our pillows at night. Finkl, delicate pampered Finkl, lost her speech in her great grief. Her mother was no longer living and Reb Falik, too, didn't survive long. Finkl inherited all his wealth, but what use was money? She refused to hear of anyone.

Suddenly we heard that Finkl was going to marry Pelte. The news came on a wintry Thursday evening, and a chill went through everyone. "The man is of the devil!" my mother cried out. "Such a one should be ridden out of town." We youngsters were petrified. I used to sleep by myself but that night I crawled into bed with my sister. I was in a fever. Later we learned that the match had been arranged by a man who was a bit of this and a bit of that and a general nuisance. It was said that he had borrowed a Gemorra from Pelte and found a hundred-ruble note among its pages. Pelte had a habit of hiding paper money in books. What one thing had to do with the other I didn't know—I was still a child then. But what difference does it make? Finkl consented. When God wants to punish someone, He deprives him of reason. People ran to her, they tore their hair trying to dissuade her, but she wouldn't change her mind. The wedding was on the Sabbath after Shevuoth. The canopy was set up before the synagogue, as is the custom when a virgin gets married, but it seemed to all of us that we were attending a funeral. I was in one of the two rows of girls who stand holding candles in their hands. It was a summer evening and the air was still, but when the groom was led past, the flames began to flicker. I shook with fear. The fiddles started to play a wedding tune, but it was a wail, not music that they made. The bass viol mourned. I wouldn't wish anyone ever to hear the like. To tell you the truth, I'd rather not go on with the story. It might give you nightmares, and I myself don't feel up to it. What? You do want to hear more. Very well. You will have to take me home. Tonight I won't walk home alone.

II

Where was I? Yes, Finkl got married. She looked more like a corpse than a bride. The bridesmaids had to support her. Who knows? Maybe she had changed her mind. But was it her fault? It was all from Above. I once heard of a bride who ran away from under the canopy. But not Finkl. She would rather be burned alive than humiliate anyone.

Need I tell you how it all ended? Can't you guess yourselves? May all the enemies of Israel come to such an end. I must say that this time he didn't pull his usual tricks. On the contrary, he tried to comfort her. But he gave off a black melancholy. She tried to lose herself in household duties. And young women came to visit her. There was a constant going back and forth, as with a woman in confinement. They told stories, they knitted, they sewed and asked riddles, anything to distract Finkl. Some even began to hint that perhaps it wasn't such an impossible match. He was rich, and a scholar too. Mightn't he become human living with her? It was reckoned that Finkl would become pregnant and have a baby and get used to her lot. Aren't there many unsuitable marriages in the world! But it wasn't fated that way. Finkl miscarried and had a hemorrhage. They had to bring a doctor from Zamoscz. He advised her to keep herself occupied. She did not become pregnant again, and then her troubles began. He tormented her, everybody knew that. But when she was asked: "What is he doing to you?" she would only say, "Nothing." "If he does nothing to you, why do you have such brown and blue rings around your eyes? And why do you go about like a lost soul?" But she would only say: "I don't know why myself."

How long did this go on? Longer than anyone expected. We all thought she wouldn't last more than a year, but she suffered for three and a half years. She faded like a light. Relatives tried to send her to the hot baths, but she refused to go. Things reached such a pass that people began to pray for her end. One mustn't say it, but death is preferable to such a life. She, too, cursed herself. Before she died, she sent for the rabbi to have him write her will. She probably wanted to leave her wealth for charitable purposes. What else? Leave it to her murderer? But again fate intervened. Some girl suddenly cried "Fire!" and everyone ran to look after his own things. It turned out that there had been no fire. "Why did you cry 'fire'?" the girl was asked. And she explained that it wasn't she who had shouted, but that something inside her had cried out. Meanwhile Finkl died, and Pelte inherited her property. Now he was the richest man in town, but he haggled over the cost of the grave till he got it for half-price.

Until then he hadn't been called Wife Killer. A man is twice widowed—such things happen. But after this he was always called Pelte the Wife Killer. *Cheder* boys pointed at him: "Here comes the Wife Killer." After the Seven Days of Mourning, the rabbi sent for him. "Reb Pelte," he said, "you are now the richest man in Turbin. Half the stores in the market place belong to you. With God's help you have become great. It is time you changed your ways. How long will you live apart from everyone else?" But no words impressed him. Talk of one thing to him, and he answers something entirely different; or he bites his lips and says nothing—

you might as well talk to the wall. When the rabbi saw that it was a waste of time, he let him go.

For a time he was silent. He began to bake his own bread again, and to collect chips and cones and dung for fuel. He was shunned like the plague. He seldom came to the synagogue. Everybody was glad not to see him. On Thursdays he went around with his book to collect debts or interest. He had everything written down and never forgot a thing. If a storekeeper said that he hadn't the money to pay him and asked him to come some other time, he wouldn't go but stayed right there, staring with his bulging eyes, till the storekeeper got tired of it and gave him his last cent. The rest of the week he hid away somewhere in his kitchen. At least ten years passed this way, perhaps eleven; I don't remember any more. He must have been in his late fifties, or perhaps in his sixties. Nobody tried to arrange a match for him.

And then something happened, and this is what I want to tell you about. As I live, one could write a book about it; but I will make it short. In Turbin there lived a woman who was called Zlateh the Bitch. Some called her Zlateh the Cossack. From her nicknames you can guess for yourselves what sort of a person she was. It is not right to gossip about the dead, but the truth must be told—she was the lowest and meanest sort. She was a fishwife and her hus-

band had been a fisherman. It's shameful to tell
what she did in her youth. She was a slut—
everyone knew that. She had a bastard somewhere. Her husband used to work in the poorhouse. There he beat and robbed the sick. How
he suddenly got to be a fisherman I don't know,
but that makes no difference. Fridays they used
to stand in the market place with a basket of
fish and curse everyone, whether they bought
or not. Curses tumbled from her mouth as from
a torn sack. If someone complained that she
cheated on the weight, she would grab a fish by
the tail and strike out. She tore the wig from
the head of more than one woman. Once she
was accused of stealing, so she went to the rabbi
and falsely swore before black candles and the
board on which the dead are washed that she
was innocent. Her husband was named Eber,
a strange name; he came from far off in Poland.
He died and she became a widow. She was so
wicked that all through the funeral she howled,
"Eber, don't forget to take along all troubles."
After the Seven Days of Mourning, she again
sold fish in the market place. Since she was a
shrew and abused everyone, people taunted her.
One woman said to her, "Aren't you going to
remarry, Zlateh?" And she answered, "Why
not? I'm still a tasty dish." Yet she was already
an old hag. "Whom will you marry, Zlateh?"
people asked her, and she thought a moment
and said, "Pelte."

The women thought she was joking and they laughed. But it was no joke, as you will soon hear.

III

One woman said to her, "But he is a Wife Killer!" And Zlateh answered, "If he is a Wife Killer, I am a worse Husband Killer. Eber wasn't my first husband." Who could tell how many she had before him? She wasn't a native of Turbin—the devil brought her from somewhere on the other side of the Vistula. Nobody paid any attention to what she said, but hardly a week passed before everybody heard that Zlateh hadn't been talking at random. Nobody knew whether she sent a matchmaker or arranged the match herself, but the marriage was going through. The whole town laughed—a fitting pair, falsehood and wickedness. Everybody said the same, "If Finkl were alive and saw who was inheriting her place, she would die of grief." Tailors' apprentices and seamstresses at once began to wager who would outlast whom. The apprentices said that nobody was a match for Pelte the Wife Killer, and the seamstresses argued that Zlateh was younger by some years and that not even Pelte had a chance once she opened her mouth. Anyway, the wedding took place. I wasn't there. You know that when a widower takes a widow, there's little fuss. But others who were there had lots of fun. The bride was all decked out. On Saturday she came to the women's gallery in the synagogue wearing a hat with a feather. She couldn't read. That Saturday I happened to take a new bride to the synagogue, and Zlateh stood right near me. She took Finkl's seat. She talked and jabbered all the time so that I didn't know what to do with myself for shame. And do you know what she said? She abused her husband. "He won't last long with me around," she said; just like that. A bitch—no doubt about it.

For some time nobody talked about them. After all, a whole town can't always bother with such scum. Then suddenly there was an outcry again. Zlateh had hired a maid, a little woman who had been abandoned by her husband. The maid started telling horrible stories. Pelte and Zlateh were at war—not just they, that is, but their stars. All sorts of things happened. Once Zlateh stood in the middle of the room and the chandelier fell down; it missed her by an inch. "The Wife Killer is at his tricks again," she said. "I'll show him something." The next day Pelte was walking in the market place; he slipped and fell into a ditch and nearly broke his neck. Every day something new happened. One time the soot in the chimney caught fire, and the entire house almost burned down; another time the cornice of the wardrobe fell and barely missed Pelte's skull. Everybody could see plainly that one or the other would have to go. It is written somewhere that every man is followed by devils—a thousand on the left and ten thousand on the right. We had a *malamed* in town, a certain Reb Itche the Slaughtered—that's what he was called—a very fine man who knew all about "those" matters. He said that this was a case of war between "them." At first things were fairly quiet; that is, people talked, but the unfortunate couple didn't say a thing. But in the end, Zlateh came running to the rabbi all atremble. "Rabbi," she shouted, "I can't stand it any more. Just think of it: I prepared dough in a trough and covered it with a pillow. I wanted to get up early to bake bread. In the middle of the night I see—the dough is on my bed. It's his work, Rabbi. He's made up his mind to finish me." At that time Reb Eisele Teumim, a true saint, was rabbi in the town. He couldn't believe his own ears. "Why should a man play such tricks?" he asked. "Why? You tell me why!" she answered. "Rabbi, send for him, let him tell it himself." The *shames* was sent and he brought Pelte. Naturally, he denied everything. "She is giving me a bad name," he cried. "She wants to get rid of me and get my money. She cast a spell to make water collect in the cellar. I went down there to get a piece of rope and was nearly drowned. Besides, she brought on a plague of mice." Pelte declared on oath that at night Zlateh whistled in bed, and that as soon as she started whistling there was a squeaking and a rushing of mice from all the holes. He pointed to a scar over his eyebrow and said that a mouse had bitten him there. When the rabbi realized whom he had to deal with, he said, "Take my advice and get divorced. It will be better for both of you." "The rabbi is right," Zlateh said. "I am willing, this very minute, but let him give me a settlement of half the property." "I won't give you the price of a pinch of snuff!" Pelte shouted. "What's more, you will pay me a fine." He grabbed his cane and wanted to strike her. He was held back with difficulty. When the rabbi saw that he would get nowhere in this case, he said, "Go your ways and leave me to my studies." So they went away.

From that time on the town had no rest. It was frightening to pass by their house. The shutters were always closed, even in the day time. Zlateh stopped selling fish, and all they did was fight. Zlateh was a giant of a woman. She used to go to the landowners' ponds and help spread the nets. She would get up in the middle of the night in winter, and in the worst frosts she never used a fire-pot. "The devil won't take me," she'd say. "I'm never cold." And now she suddenly aged. Her face blackened and was wrinkled like that of a woman of seventy. She started coming to strangers' houses to ask for advice. Once she came to my mother—peace be on her—and begged to be allowed to stay over-night. My mother looked at her as one demented. "What happened?" she asked. "I'm afraid of him," Zlateh said. "He wants to get rid of me. He makes winds in the house." She said that though the windows were sealed outside with clay and inside with straw, strong winds blew in her bedroom. She also swore that her bed would rise beneath her, and that Pelte spent half the nights in the outhouse—if you'll pardon the expression. "What does he do there so long?" my mother asked. "He has a mistress there," Zlateh said. I happened to be in the alcove and heard all this. Pelte must have had dealings with the Unclean Ones. My mother shuddered. "Listen to me, Zlateh," she said, "give him the 'dozen lines' and run for your life. If they were to give me my weight in gold, I wouldn't live under the same roof with anyone like that." But a Cossack never changes. "He won't get rid of me just like that," Zlateh said. "Let him give me a settlement." In the end, my mother made up a bed for her on the bench. We didn't shut an eye that night. Before dawn she got up and left. Mother couldn't fall asleep again and lit a taper in the kitchen. "You know," she said to me, "I have a feeling that she won't get out of his hands alive. Well, it won't be a big loss." But Zlateh wasn't Finkl. She didn't give up so easily, as you will soon hear.

IV

What did she do? I don't know. People told all sorts of stories, but you can't believe everything. We had an old peasant woman in town, Cunegunde. She must have been a hundred years old, maybe older. Everybody knew that she was a witch. Her whole face was covered with warts, and she walked almost on all fours. Her hut was at the end of town, on the sand, and it was full of all kinds of animals: rabbits and guinea pigs, cats and dogs, and all kinds of vermin. Birds flew in and out of the windows. The place stank. But Zlateh became a frequent visitor and spent whole days there. The woman knew how to pour wax. If a peasant was sick, he would come to her, and she'd pour molten wax which formed all sorts of strange figures and showed what the sickness came from—though it did little good.

As I was saying, people in town said this Cunegunde taught Zlateh a charm. Anyway, Pelte became a changed man, soft as butter. She wanted him to transfer the house to her name, so he hired a team of horses and went to town to register the transfer. Then she started meddling in his stores. Now it was she who went about on Thursdays with the interest and rent book. She asked for increases right away. The storekeepers cried that they were losing their shirts, so she said, "In that case you can go begging." A meeting was held, and Pelte was called. He was so weak that he could barely walk. He was completely deaf. "There is nothing I can do," he said. "Everything belongs to her. If she wants to, she can drive me out of the house." She would have, too, but he hadn't transferred everything to her yet. He was still bargaining with her. Neighbors said that she was starving him. He used to go into houses and beg for a piece of bread. His hands shook. Everybody saw that Zlateh was having her way. Some were glad—he was being punished for Finkl. Others argued that Zlateh would ruin the town. It's not a small matter when so much property gets into the hands of such a beast. She began to build and to dig. She brought craftsmen from Yanov and they started measuring the streets. She put on a wig, with silver combs, and she carried a purse and a parasol, like a real aristocrat. She burst into homes early in the morning, before the beds were made, and she pounded on tables and shouted, "I'll throw you out with your junk. I'll have you locked up in the Yanov jail! I'll make beggars out of you!" Poor people tried to fawn on her, but she wouldn't even listen. Then people realized that it isn't wise to wish for a new king.

One afternoon the door of the poorhouse opened, and Pelte came in, dressed like a beggar. The man in charge of the poorhouse turned pale as a ghost. "Reb Pelte," he exclaimed, "what are you doing here?" "I came to stay here," Pelte answered. "My wife has thrown me out." To make a long story short, Pelte had transferred all his possessions to Zlateh, everything, down to the last thread, and then she chased him out. "But how does one do a thing like that?" he was asked. "Don't even ask," he answered. "She fixed me! I barely came out alive." The poorhouse was in an uproar. Some cursed Pelte. "As if the rich don't have enough as it is—now they come to eat the food of the poor," they cried. Others pretended sympathy. In short, Pelte was given a bundle of straw to spread in the corner, and he lay down. The whole town came running to see the sight. I, too, was curious and ran to see. He sat on the floor like a mourner and stared at everybody with his bulging eyes. People asked him, "Why do you sit here, Reb Pelte, what happened to all your power?" At first he didn't answer at all, as if they weren't talking to him, and later he said, "She isn't finished with me yet." "What will you do to her?" the beggars jeered. They made a laughing-stock of him. But don't jump at conclusions. You know the old saying: He laughs best who laughs last.

For several weeks Zlateh was a regular demon. She turned the whole town upside down. Right in the middle of the market place, near the stores, she had a pit dug and hired men to mix lime. Logs were brought and heaps of brick were piled up so that no one could pass. Roofs were torn down and a notary came from Yanov to make a list of all her tenants' belongings. Zlateh bought a carriage and a team of fiery horses, and she went riding every afternoon. She started wearing shoes with pointed tips and let her hair grow. She also began to pal around with the *goyim* of the Christian streets. She bought two vicious dogs, regular killers, so that it was dangerous to pass by her house. She stopped selling fish. What did she need it for? But out of habit, she had to have fish around, so she filled bathtubs in her house and stocked them with carp and pike. She even kept a big tub full of *treif* fish, and lobsters and frogs and eels. It was rumored in town that she would become an apostate any day. Some said that on Pesach the priest had come to her house to sprinkle it with holy water. People feared that she might inform on the community—someone like that is capable of anything.

Suddenly, she came running to the rabbi. "Rabbi," she said, "send for Pelte. I want a divorce." "What do you want a divorce for?" the rabbi asked her. "Do you want to remarry?" "I don't know," she said. "Maybe yes and maybe no. But I don't want to be the wife of a Wife Killer. I'm willing to compensate him with something." The rabbi sent for Pelte and he came crawling. Everybody in town stood outside the rabbi's house. Poor Pelte, he consented to everything. His hands shook as in a fever. Reb

Moishe the Scribe sat down to write out the divorce. I remember him as if this happened yesterday. He was a small man and had a tic. He ruled the paper with his penknife, and then he wiped the goose quill on his skull cap. The witnesses were instructed how to sign divorce. My husband, peace be on him, was one of the witnesses because he wrote a good hand. Zlateh sat comfortably on a chair and sucked candy. And, yes, I forgot to mention it, she put down two hundred rubles. Pelte recognized them—he had had a habit of marking his money. The rabbi ordered silence, but Zlateh boasted to the women that she was considering marrying a "possessor," but that "as long as the Wife Killer is my husband, I am not sure of staying alive." When she said this she laughed so that everybody outside heard her.

When everything was ready, the rabbi began questioning the couple. I still remember his words. "Hear me, Paltiel, son of Schneour Zalman"—that was the name by which Pelte was called up to the reading of the Torah—"do you want to divorce your wife?" He said something more, from the *Gemorra,* but I can't say it as he did. "Say 'yes,'" he ordered Pelte. "Say 'yes' once, not twice." Pelte said "yes." We could hardly hear him. "Hear me, Zlateh Golde, daughter of Yehuda Treitel, do you want to divorce your husband, Paltiel?" "Yes!" Zlateh shouted, and as she said this she swayed and fell to the floor in a faint. I saw this myself, and I tell you the truth; I felt my brain bursting in my head. I thought I'd collapse too. There was a great outcry and commotion. Everybody rushed to revive her. They poured water on her and stuck pins into her and rubbed her with vinegar and pulled her hair. Azriel the Healer came running and cupped her then and there. She still breathed, but it wasn't the same Zlateh. May God preserve us. Her mouth was twisted to one side and the spittle ran out of it; her eyes were rolled up and her nose was white, like that of a corpse. The women who stood near, heard her mumble, "The Wife Killer! He overcame me!" These were her last words.

At the funeral there was almost a riot. Now Pelte was again on his high horse. Beside his own property he now also had her wealth. Her jewelry alone was worth a fortune. The burial society wanted a big sum, but Pelte wouldn't budge. They shouted, they warned, they abused him. They threatened him with excommunication. Might as well talk to the wall! "I won't give a penny, let her rot," he said. They would have left her lying around, too, but it was summertime and there was a heat wave just then, and people feared an epidemic. In short, some women performed the rites—what other choice was there? The pall-bearers refused to carry her, so a wagon was hired. She was buried right near the fence, among the stillbirths. All the same, Pelte said *kaddish* after her—this he did.

From then on the Wife Killer remained alone.

People were so afraid of him, they avoided passing by his house. Mothers of pregnant young women did not allow his name to be mentioned, unless they first put on two aprons. *Cheder* boys fingered their fringes before pronouncing his name. And nothing came of all the construction and remodelling. The bricks were carried off, the lime was stolen. The carriage and its team of horses disappeared—he must have sold them. The water in the bathtubs dried up, and the fish died. There was a cage with a parrot in the house. It squawked, "I'm hungry"—it could talk Yiddish—until at last it starved to death. Pelte had the shutters nailed tight and never opened them again. He didn't even go out to collect the pennies from the storekeepers. All day he lay on his bench and snored, or simply dozed. At night he'd go out to collect chips. Once each week, they sent him two loaves of bread from the bakery, and the baker's wife would buy him some onions, garlic, radishes and, on occasion, a piece of dry cheese. He never ate meat. He never came to the synagogue on Saturdays. There was no broom in his house and the dirt gathered in heaps. Mice ran about even during the day and spider webs hung from the rafters. The roof leaked and wasn't repaired. The walls rotted and caved in. Every few weeks it was rumored that things were not well with the Wife Killer, that he was sick, or dying. The burial society rubbed its hands in anticipation. But nothing happened. He outlived everyone.

He lived so long that people in Turbin began to hint that he might live forever. Why not? Maybe he had some special kind of blessing, or the Angel of Death forgot him. Anything can happen.

Rest assured that he was not forgotten by the Angel of Death. But when that happened I was no longer in Turbin. He must have been a hundred years old, maybe older. After the funeral his entire house was turned upside down, but nothing of value was found. The chests had rotted away. The gold and silver were gone. The money and notes turned to dust the minute a breeze touched them. All the digging in the heaps of rubbish was wasted. The Wife Killer had outlived everything: his wives, his enemies, his money, his property, his generation. All that was left after him—may God forgive me for saying so—was a heap of dust.

Translated by Shlomo Katz

BY THE LIGHT OF
MEMORIAL CANDLES

I

As the darkness grew more intense, so did the frost. In the study house, though the clay oven had been heated, frost patterned the windows, and icicles hung from the frames. The beadle had extinguished the oil lamps, but two memorial candles, one tall, the other short, remained burning in the *menorah* at the east wall. The short one, burning since the day before, had grown thick with melted tallow. From the memorial candles, it is said, one can surmise the fate of those in whose memory they were kindled; the flames flicker and sputter when the soul of the departed has not found peace. And as the flames quiver, everything else appears to do so, the posts of the reading table, the rafters supporting the ceiling, the chandeliers on their chains, and even the Holy Ark, carved with lions and tablets. In summer, a fly or moth, falling into the wick, will cause the flickering; but there are no flies or moths in winter.

Benches, on three sides of the clay oven, supported wandering beggars who slept there at night. But tonight, although it was past midnight, they could not fall asleep. One of them, a short, freckled man, with straw-colored hair, a round red beard, and angry eyes, cut his toenails with a pocket knife. Another, fleshy-faced, calf-eyed, with white hair curling like wood shavings over his huge head, dried his foot rags. A tall man, sooty as a stoker's shovel, roasted potatoes, the red hot coals reflecting their glow on his face. A man, husky and pock-marked, a tumor on his forehead, and a beard like dirty cotton, lay, immobile, as if paralyzed, his eyes fixed somewhere on the wall.

The man with the huge head spoke, spitting out his words as though his tongue too were oversized. He said, "How can you tell when a man has already been married? If I say I'm still a bachelor, who can say I'm not?"

"So, if you're a bachelor, what of it?" the red-haired man answered. "Do you think the most important man in town will marry his daughter to you? You're a tramp and you'll remain one; there's no escape. You'll keep on wandering across the land with your beggar's pack; like me, for example. Once I was a craftsman, a saddlemaker; I made saddles for the nobility. But after my wife died I couldn't work any longer. I was restless and had to wander off. I became a beggar."

With fingers that no longer reacted to fire, the tall man rolled a potato out of the bed of coals. "Does anyone want a bite? I'd work, if I could find a job. But no one wants carvers any more. Long ago everything came from the

carver, jewelry boxes, containers for holiday
citrus, cases for the Book of Esther. I would
carve cornices on wardrobes, headboards for
beds, door panels. Once I was invited by a town
to carve a Holy Ark for the synagogue. People
from all over the country came to look at it. I
stayed there for two years. But today you buy
things readymade, with a few decorations thrown
in. It wasn't I, but my father, may he rest in
peace, who wanted to be a carver. For five generations back our family were carvers. But
what's the use? It's a dying craft. Well, there
was nothing to do but beg."

For a while no one spoke. The red-bearded
beggar, having cut his last toenail, wrapped his
nail shavings and two splinters from the bench
in a piece of paper, and threw them into the
fire. On the day of reckoning, the two splinters
would be witnesses to the fact that he had not
desecrated any parts of his body by casting them
into the rubbish. Then he stared at the beggar
with the tumor.

"Hey you, whatever-your-name-is, over there!
How did you get that way?"

The man with the tumor made no response.

"What's the matter—are you mute?"

"I am not mute."

"Then why don't you speak? Does it cost anything?"

"If one is silent, one is silent."

"A word," the carver remarked, "is like a gold
coin to him."

The red-bearded beggar began to whet his pocket knife on an edge of the oven.

"Will you be here for the Sabbath?"

"Of course."

"Then we can talk later. Pretty cold, eh? The roofs are cracking. I've heard that the entire winter sowing has frozen under the snow. This means famine."

"Oh, what won't people say! It's never cold under the snow. Even before the grain has split in the earth, the landowners have sold it. It's the grain merchants who lose out."

"What do they lose? When the harvest is bad, prices go wild, and that makes profits even bigger. The poor man is the one who always suffers most."

"Well, what do you expect? Everyone can't be rich; some must be poor too," the red-beard argued. "But surely the man doomed to be poor must be pitied. Not that I mind being hungry on weekdays—but if a miser boards you on the Sabbath, you're out of luck! When the Sabbath is scanty, you're hungry all week. Where I come from, the Sabbath overnight roasts are fat ones. But here everything is lean, even the pudding."

The man with the tumor suddenly grew talkative. "All the same one keeps from starving. You eat a lot, or you eat a little. As they say, the stomach stretches. If I get a piece of bread and an onion, I'm happy."

"One can't walk very far on bread and onion." The man with the tumor sat up.

"You just start your feet walking and they do the rest. When you're home, you do as you please; but as soon as you've left home, you have to keep moving. in one town today, in another tomorrow. A day here, a night there. Who watches over you? I used to make a pretty good living. I had a trade for which there is always a demand. I come from Tsivkev and I was the gravedigger there. It may be a small place, but people die everywhere. I was a gravedigger for the old, the young—the hell-beadle. There was a burial society in our town, but its members were busy in the villages all week long, buying pig bristles from the peasants to make brushes. The burden was entirely mine. I had to cleanse the bodies and sew the shrouds. I lived in a hut opposite the cemetery. My wife became sick. One day I realized she would soon die. She took a little soup and then it was all over. For forty years, like a pair of pigeons, we had lived together. Suddenly she lay down and died. With my own hands I buried her. People hate a gravedigger. Is he to blame? I had no wish to harm anyone. For my part, people can live forever. But that's how it is. Well, when my own wife died, I even had to bury her.

"Corpses, they would say, roam the graveyard at night. One heard of the ghost of this person, that person, little fires, phantoms. But for thirty years I was a gravedigger and saw nothing. I walked into the synagogue in the middle of the night, but no voice ever called me to the reading table. When you die, everything's over. Even if there is a hereafter, a corpse in this world is nothing but a pile of flesh and bones.

"Once in a while, when a stranger died in our town, the body was left in the cleansing room overnight. Since I was the watchman, I would light two candles at its head and chant psalms. But how long can you chant psalms? My lids would begin to droop; I'd lie down on the bench and doze. The wind would blow out the candles and I'd be alone in the dark with the corpse. Once I forgot to take along my pillow stuffed with hay. I couldn't go home because it was raining and I didn't want to wake my wife, so, forgive me for saying so, I took the body, and placed it beneath my head. As sure as I'm here in the synagogue, it's no lie."

"It isn't everyone who could do that," the red-bearded man said.

"I'd go mad with fear," said the calf-eyed beggar with the huge head.

"You don't go mad so easily. Are you afraid of a slaughtered goose? A human corpse is like a dead goose. Why do you think the corpse needs to be watched? To keep the mice away.

"As I said, I made a good living. But when my wife died, I grew lonely. We had no children. The matchmakers had some suggestions, but how can you let a stranger take the place of a woman you've lived with for so many years? Others might do it; I couldn't. All day long I stared at her grave. Once the matchmaker sent a woman to the hut. She began to sweep the floor. She was supposed to size me up, but the moment I saw her take the broom, I felt nauseated and had to send her away. Since becoming a widower, I have learned to boil a pot of potatoes in their skins. I even started to bake bread in the oven on Friday mornings. But without a wife, there's no one to talk to. Yes, I was lonely, but I had funds. I could even give alms to the poor. Charity, my brothers, is the best deed."

II

"Then why did you become a vagabond?" the red-bearded man asked.

"Shh. Don't rush. Haste makes waste. I've said already that one has nothing to fear from a corpse. But here's the story. About five years ago there was an epidemic in our county. Every year, especially in the fall, there are epidemics that kill infants. They die like flies from smallpox, measles, scarlet fever, and the croup. Once I buried eight children in a day. It's not a hard job. Shrouds aren't needed, a cotton cloth will do; you open a shallow ditch—and that's it. The cleansing doesn't amount to much either. Yes, the mothers cry, but that's how they are. But this time, it was the grown-ups who were hit by the epidemic—cholera. They had cramps in their legs; rubbing them with alcohol didn't help. They'd vomit, get diarrhea—the usual symptoms. Even the barber-healer caught it and died. The man who tried to fetch the doctor from Zamosc was overcome on the way by cramps, and died as he reached the inn. Yes, the angel of death reaped his harvest.

"I became a one-man burial society because the other members of the society were afraid to return to town. With a mute, I traveled from house to house in search of corpses, and took them away immediately, because most of our families live in one room and you can't mix the dead with the sick. It was a bad time. Since the bodies had to be cleansed and shrouds made for them, they couldn't be buried the same day. The cleansing room was filled with corpses. At night I'd light the candles and sit down to recite psalms. One night there were nine corpses, five men and four women. They were scarcely covered by the sheets. In an epidemic, everything is upside down.

"And do you know that those who die of cholera make strange faces? I had to tie the chin of one young man who seemed to be laughing. But he went on laughing. One woman looked as though she were screaming. It just happened that she screamed a good deal when she was alive.

"Corpses are cold, but those who die of cholera remain warm. The forehead is hot when you touch it. On other nights I used to drop off for a bit, but I didn't sleep a wink that night.

"They say a gravedigger has no pity. Nonsense. My heart bled for the young people. Why should their years be cut short? It was raining hard outside. Although it was the month of Cheshvan, there was thunder and lightning, as in the summer. Heaven was weeping. The few graves I had dug were flooded.

"There was a seventeen-year-old girl, a shoe-maker's daughter, among the corpses, a girl already engaged. Her father, Zellig the Shoe-maker, used to mend my boots. He had three sons but he adored her, for she was his only daughter. But the whole family had become ill and I couldn't leave the corpse among them. Before taking her away, I tested her nostrils with a feather, but it didn't move. I covered her with a sack in the cleansing room. Her cheeks remained red, but in cholera, as I told you, the face of the corpse has the color of life. 'Father in heaven,' I argued, 'why do they deserve this? For years parents must wait to enjoy their children, and then before you know it the dance is over.'

"As I sang psalms, the cover on the girl seemed to stir. I thought I had imagined it; corpses don't move. Again I sang psalms, and again the cover stirred. It must be clear to you men by now that I don't scare easily; nevertheless a chill ran down my spine. I reasoned with myself: a mouse or skunk must be pulling the sack. But just then the sack fell off. The corpse raised its head. I heard her gasp, 'Water, water!' That's exactly what she said.

"Now I know what a fool I was; she was still

alive. The dead aren't thirsty. She must have been in what they call a cataleptic trance. But at the time I was so terrified that I ran out of the cleansing room, shouting for help. I ran so fast, I almost broke my legs. I kept shouting, but no one heard me. The cemetery was far from town and the rain was pouring. I called, 'Hear, O Israel,' and anything else that came into my head. I just made it to the edge of town, but everyone was afraid to open up when I knocked on the shutters. They thought I was mad, I guess. Finally a few butchers and some coachmen woke up and came with me, lanterns in hand. On the way back to the cemetery they kept teasing. 'Getz,' they said—my name is Getz—, 'you should be ashamed of yourself. It's only fright that makes you see things. Others will laugh at you.' Although they played tough, they themselves were shaken.

"In our town, the gutters are flooded when it rains. We waded in water up to our knees. It's not too clever to catch a cold during an epidemic. We were soaked.

"When we entered the cleansing room we found the girl lying there with arms outspread and no cover. They rubbed her, shook her, blew at her, but she was really dead now. They began to make fun of me and to scold. Butchers will always be butchers. I swore that she had been covered with a sack and had thrown it off when she tried to sit up, but they told me it had only seemed that way. One called it a mirage, another a vision, a dream, God knows what. They made me look foolish. But there wasn't much time to argue, for everyone had to return home. I drew the girl's arms and legs together, covered her with a sack and once more started singing psalms. But now I was jumpy. My heart was like a drum. I swallowed a little whisky from a bottle I had handy, but it didn't help. I kept one eye on the psalms, the other on the corpses. If something like this could happen, how could one be sure of anything? The wind tried to blow out the candles. I had a match box with me, and I didn't mean to be left in the dark, not for a moment. I was happy when morning came.

"I forgot to mention that we didn't tell the girl's parents, for they would have been horrified. And, who knows, maybe she could have been saved. But it was too late. The next day I was ready to leave town, but you can't leave in the midst of an epidemic. I no longer wanted to watch corpses by myself, so I hired the mute to keep me company. True, he slept all the time, but he was a human being.

"Now each grave I dug, each corpse I cleansed, worried me. I kept thinking of that girl, of her sitting up and whispering, 'Water, water!' When I slept, she was in my dreams. Now I had all sorts of ideas. Who knows? Maybe she wasn't the only one. Maybe other corpses had wakened in their graves. I was sorry I had buried my wife the day she died. Never, until then, had I been afraid to look a corpse in the face. They

say you forget all you know when you look at
the face of a corpse; but what did I know? Nothing! But now, when a corpse was brought in, I
didn't look at it. It always seemed that the
corpse was winking, trying to say something
and not being able to. Winter, meanwhile, was
howling and whistling outside, like seven witches
that had hanged themselves. And I was alone,
because the mute had been unwilling to stay.
But one doesn't leave a job easily. At night, on
my bed, I kept turning and twisting, unable to
sleep.

"One night I felt a scratching in my ear, not
from without, but within. I awoke and heard
my wife. She whispered: 'Getz!' I must have
dreamt it; the dead don't talk. But the ear is
delicate. I can stand all kinds of pain, but not
a tickle in my ear. The ear, you know, is near
the brain. The wind had grown quiet. Now,
men, I will tell you something. I lit a candle and
dressed. I stuffed a sack with linen, a coat, and
a loaf of bread, and left, in the middle of the
night, with no good-bys. The town owed me a
month's pay, but it didn't matter. I didn't even
take leave of my wife's grave, which I was supposed to do. I left everything, and I went off."

"Without money?"

"I had a few rubles in a little bag."

"Scared?" the red-bearded beggar asked.

"Not scared, but upset. I meant to become a
merchant, but somehow I couldn't keep my
mind on business. What does a man need by

himself? A slice of bread and a glass of water. People are good to one."

"And your ear? Does your wife still call?"

"No one calls. My ear has cotton in it."

"Why cotton?"

"To keep it from catching cold. No other reason."

The beggars were silent. In the stillness, one heard the coals rustling in the oven. The first to speak was the beggar with the huge head.

"If it had happened to me, I'd have dropped dead."

"If you're destined to live, you live."

"Maybe, after all, it was your wife," said the carver.

"And maybe you're the Rabbi of Lublin," answered the gravedigger.

"She might have wanted to tell you something," the red-bearded man said.

"What could she want to tell me? I never took another in her place."

The short memorial candle flickered and went out. In the study house, the light grew dimmer. An odor of tallow and burnt wick drifted across from the *menorah* on the east wall. Slowly and silently, the beggars lay down on their benches.

Translated by Martha Glicklich
and Elaine Gottlieb

THE MIRROR

I

There is a kind of net that is as old as Methuselah, as soft as a cobweb and as full of holes, yet it has retained its strength to this day. When a demon wearies of chasing after yesterdays or of going round in circles on a windmill, he can install himself inside a mirror. There he waits like a spider in its web, and the fly is certain to be caught. God has bestowed vanity on the female, particularly on the rich, the pretty, the barren, the young, who have much time and little company.

I discovered such a woman in the village of Krashnik. Her father dealt in timber; her husband floated the logs to Danzig; grass was growing on her mother's grave. The daughter lived in an old house, among oaken cupboards, leather-lined coffers, and books bound in silk. She had two servants, an old one that was deaf and a young one who carried on with a fiddler. The other Krashnik housewives wore men's boots, ground buckwheat on millstones, plucked feathers, cooked broths, bore children, and attended funerals. Needless to say, Zirel, beautiful and well-educated—she had been brought up in Cracow—had nothing to talk about with her small-town neighbors. And so she preferred to read her German song book and embroider Moses and Ziporah, David and Bathsheba, Ahasuereus and Queen Esther on canvas. The pretty dresses her husband brought her hung in the closet. Her pearls and diamonds lay in her jewel box. No one ever saw her silk slips, her lace petticoats, nor her red hair which was hidden under her wig, not even her husband. For when could they be seen? Certainly not during the day, and at night it is dark.

But Zirel had an attic which she called her boudoir, and where hung a mirror as blue as water on the point of freezing. The mirror had a crack in the middle and it was set in a golden frame which was decorated with snakes, knobs, roses, and adders. In front of the mirror lay a bearskin and close beside it was a chair with armrests of ivory and a cushioned seat. What could be more pleasant than to sit naked in this chair, and rest one's feet on the bearskin, and contemplate oneself? Zirel had much to gaze at. Her skin was white as satin, her breasts as full as wineskins, her hair fell across her shoulders, and her legs were as slender as a hind's. She would sit for hours on end delighting in her beauty. The door fastened and bolted, she would imagine that it opened to admit either a prince or a hunter or a knight or a poet. For everything hidden must be revealed, each secret longs to be disclosed, each love yearns to be betrayed, everything sacred must be desecrated. Heaven and earth conspire that all good beginnings should come to a bad end.

Well, once I learned of the existence of this luscious little tidbit, I determined that she would be mine. All that was required was a little patience. One summer day, as she sat staring at the nipple on her left breast, she caught sight of me in the mirror—there I was, black as tar, long as a shovel, with donkey's ears, a ram's horns, a frog's mouth, and a goat's beard. My eyes were all pupil. She was so surprised that she forgot to be frightened. Instead of crying, "Hear, O Israel," she burst out laughing.

"My, how ugly you are," she said.

"My, how beautiful you are," I replied.

She was pleased with my compliment. "Who are you?" she asked.

"Fear not," I said. "I am an imp, not a demon. My fingers have no nails, my mouth has no teeth, my arms stretch like licorice, my horns are as pliable as wax. My power lies in my tongue; I am a fool by trade, and I have come to cheer you up because you are alone."

"Where were you before?"

"In the bedroom behind the stove where the cricket chirps and the mouse rustles, between a dried wreath and a faded willow branch."

"What did you do there?"

"I looked at you."

"Since when?"

"Since your wedding night."

"What did you eat?"

"The fragrance of your body, the glow of your hair, the light of your eyes, the sadness of your face."

"Oh, you flatterer!" she cried. "Who are you? What are you doing here? Where do you come from? What is your errand?"

I made up a story. My father, I said, was a goldsmith and my mother a succubus; they copulated on a bundle of rotting rope in a cellar and I was their bastard. For some time I lived in a settlement of devils on Mount Seir where I inhabited a mole's hole. But when it was learned that my father was human I was driven out. From then on I had been homeless. She-devils avoided me because I reminded them of the sons of Adam; the daughters of Eve saw in me Satan. Dogs barked at me, children wept when they saw me. Why were they afraid? I harmed no one. My only desire was to gaze at beautiful women—to gaze and converse with them.

"Why converse? The beautiful aren't always wise."

"In Paradise the wise are the footstools of the beautiful."

"My teacher taught me otherwise."

"What did your teacher know? The writers of books have the brains of a flea; they merely parrot each other. Ask me when you want to know something. Wisdom extends no further than the first heaven. From there on everything is lust. Don't you know that angels are headless? The Seraphim play in the sand like children; the Cherubim can't count; the Aralim chew their cud before the throne of Glory. God himself is jovial. He spends his time pulling Leviathan by the tail and being licked by the Wild Ox; or else he tickles the Shekhinah, causing her to lay myriads of eggs each day, and each egg is a star."

"Now I know you're making fun of me."

"If that's not the truth may a funny bone grow on my nose. It's a long time since I squandered my quota of lies. I have no alternative but to tell the truth."

"Can you beget children?"

"No, my dear. Like the mule I am the last of a line. But this does not blunt my desire. I lie only with married women, for good actions are my sins; my prayers are blasphemies; spite is my bread; arrogance, my wine; pride, the marrow of my bones. There is only one other thing I can do besides chatter."

This made her laugh. Then she said: "My mother didn't bring me up to be a devil's whore. Away with you, or I'll have you exorcised."

"Why bother," I said. "I'll go. I don't force myself on anyone. *Auf wiedersehen*."

I faded away like mist.

II

For seven days Zirel absented herself from her boudoir. I dozed inside the mirror. The net had been spread; the victim was ready. I knew she was curious. Yawning, I considered my next step. Should I seduce a rabbi's daughter? deprive a bridegroom of his manhood? plug up the synagogue chimney? turn the Sabbath wine into vinegar? give an elflock to a virgin? enter a ram's horn on Rosh Hashana? make a cantor hoarse? An imp never lacks for things to do, particularly during the Days of Awe when even the fish in the water tremble. And then as I sat dreaming of moon juice and turkey seeds, she entered. She looked for me, but could not see me. She stood in front of the mirror but I didn't show myself.

"I must have been imagining," she murmured. "It must have been a daydream."

She took off her nightgown and stood there naked. I knew that her husband was in town and that he had been with her the night before although she had not gone to the ritual bath—but as the Talmud puts it, "a woman would rather have one measure of debauchery than ten of modesty." Zirel, daughter of Roize Glike, missed me, and her eyes were sad. She is mine, mine, I thought. The Angel of Death stood ready with his rod; a zealous little devil busied himself preparing the cauldron for her in hell; a sinner, promoted to stoker, collected the kindling wood. Everything was prepared—the snow drift and the live coals, the hook for her tongue and the pliers for her breasts, the mouse that would eat her liver and the worm that would gnaw her bladder. But my little charmer suspected nothing. She stroked her left breast, and then her right. She looked at her belly, examined her thighs, scrutinized her toes. Would she read her book? trim her nails? comb her hair? Her husband had brought her perfumes from Lenczyc, and she smelled of rosewater and carnations. He had presented her with a coral necklace which hung around her neck. But what is Eve without a serpent? And what is God without Lucifer? Zirel was full of desire. Like a harlot she summoned me with her eyes. With quivering lips she uttered a spell:

> *Swift is the wind,*
> *Deep the ditch,*
> *Sleek black cat,*
> *Come within reach.*
> *Strong is the lion,*
> *Dumb the fish,*
> *Reach from the silence,*
> *And take your dish.*

As she uttered the last word, I appeared. Her face lit up.

"So you're here."

"I was away," I said, "but I have returned."

"Where have you been?"

"To never-never land. I was at Rahab the Harlot's palace in the garden of the golden birds near the castle of Asmodeus."

"As far as that?"

"If you don't believe me, my jewel, come with me. Sit on my back, and hold on to my horns, and I'll spread my wings, and we'll fly together beyond the mountain peaks."

"But I don't have a thing on."

"No one dresses there."

"My husband won't have any idea where I am."

"He'll learn soon enough."

"How long a trip is it?"

"It takes less than a second."

"When will I return?"

"Those who go there don't want to return."

"What will I do there?"

"You'll sit on Asmodeus' lap and plait tresses in his beard. You'll eat almonds and drink porter; evenings you'll dance for him. Bells will be attached to your ankles, and devils will whirl with you."

"And after that?"

"If my master is pleased with you, you will be his. If not, one of his minions will take care of you."

"And in the morning?"

"There are no mornings there."

"Will you stay with me?"

"Because of you I might be given a small bone to lick."

"Poor little devil, I feel sorry for you, but I can't go. I have a husband and a father. I have gold and silver and dresses and furs. My heels are the highest in Krashnik."

"Well, then, good-by."

"Don't hurry off like that. What do I have to do?"

"Now you are being reasonable. Make some dough with the whitest of flour. Add honey, menstrual blood, and an egg with a bloodspot, a measure of pork fat, a thimbleful of suet, a goblet of libatory wine. Light a fire on the Sabbath and bake the mixture on the coals. Now call your husband to your bed and make him eat the cake you have baked. Awaken him with lies and put him to sleep with profanity. Then when he begins to snore, cut off one half of his beard and one earlock, steal his gold, burn his promissory notes, and tear up the marriage contract. After that throw your jewels under the pig butcher's window—this will be my engagement gift. Before leaving your house, throw the prayer book into the rubbish and spit on the *mezuzah*, at the precise spot where the word *Shadai* is written. Then come straight to me. I'll bear you on my wings from Krashnik to the desert. We'll fly over fields filled with toadstools, over woods inhabited by werewolves, over the ruins of Sodom where serpents are scholars, hyenas are singers, crows are preachers, and thieves are entrusted with the money for charity. There ugliness is beauty, and crooked is straight; tortures are amusement, and mockery, the height of exaltation. But hurry, for our eternity is brief."

"I'm afraid, little devil, I'm afraid."

"Everyone who goes with us is."

She wished to ask questions, to catch me in contradictions, but I made off. She pressed her lips against the mirror and met the end of my tail.

III

Her father wept; her husband tore his hair; her servants searched for her in the woodshed and in the cellar; her mother-in-law poked with a shovel in the chimney; carters and butchers hunted for her in the woods. At night, torches were lit and the voices of the searchers echoed and re-echoed: "Zirel, where are you? Zirel! Zirel!" It was suspected that she had run off to a convent, but the priest swore on the crucifix that this was not so. A wonder worker was sent for, and then a sorceress, an old Gentile woman who made wax effigies, and finally a man who located the dead or missing by means of a black mirror; a farmer lent them his blood hounds. But when I get my prey, it is reprieved by no

one. I spread my wings and we were off. Zirel
spoke to me, but I did not answer. When we
came to Sodom, I hovered a moment over Lot's
wife. Three oxen were busy licking her nose.
Lot lay in a cave with his daughters, drunk as
always.

In the vale of shadow which is known as the
world everything is subject to change. But for
us time stands still! Adam remains naked, Eve
lustful, still in the act of being seduced by the
serpent. Cain kills Abel, the flea lies with the
elephant, the flood falls from heaven, the Jews
knead clay in Egypt, Job scratches at his sore-
covered body. He will keep scratching until the
end of time, but he will find no comfort.

She wished to speak to me, but with a flutter
of wings I disappeared. I had done my errand.
I lay like a bat blinking sightless eyes on a steep
cliff. The earth was brown, the heavens yellow.
Devils stood in a circle wiggling their tails. Two
turtles were locked in an embrace, and a male
stone mounted a female stone. Shabriri and
Bariri appeared. Shabriri had assumed the
shape of a squire. He wore a pointed cap, a
curved sword; he had the legs of a goose and a
goat's beard. On his snout were glasses, and he
spoke in a German dialect. Bariri was ape, parrot, rat, bat, all at once. Shabriri bowed low and
began to chant like a jester at a wedding:

Argin, margin,
Here's a bargain.
A pretty squirrel,

Name of Zirel.
Open the door,
To love impure.

He was about to take her in his arms when
Bariri screamed, "Don't let him touch you. He
has scabs on his head, sores on his legs, and
what a woman needs he doesn't have. He acts
the great lover, but a capon is more amorous.
His father was like that also, and so was his
grandfather. Let me be your lover. I am the
grandson of the Chief Liar. In addition I am a
man of wealth and good family. My grandmother was lady-in-waiting to Machlath,
daughter of Naama. My mother had the honor
to wash Asmodeus' feet. My father, may he stay
in hell forever, carried Satan's snuffbox."

Shabriri and Bariri had grasped Zirel by the
hair, and each time they tore out a tuft. Now
Zirel saw how things were and she cried out,
"Pity, pity!"

"What's this we have here?" asked Ketev
Mariri.

"A Krashnik coquette."

"Don't they have better than that?"

"No, it's the best they've got."

"Who dragged her in?"

"A little imp."

"Let's begin."

"Help, help," Zirel moaned.

"Hang her," Wrath, the Son of Anger,

screamed. "It won't help to cry out here. Time and change have been left behind. Do what you are told; you're neither young nor old."

Zirel broke into lamentations. The sound roused Lilith from her sleep. She thrust aside Asmodeus' beard and put her head out of the cave, each of her hairs, a curling snake.

"What's wrong with the bitch?" she asked. "Why all the screaming?"

"They're working on her."

"Is that all? Add some salt."

"And skim the fat."

This fun has been going on for a thousand years, but the black gang does not weary of it. Each devil does his bit; each imp makes his pun. They pull and tear and bite and pinch. For all that, the masculine devils aren't so bad; it's the females who really enjoy themselves, commanding: Skim boiling broth with bare hands! Plait braids without using the fingers! Wash the laundry without water! Catch fish in hot sand! Stay at home and walk the streets! Take a bath without getting wet! Make butter from stones! Break the cask without spilling the wine! And all the while the virtuous women in Paradise gossip; and the pious men sit on golden chairs, stuffing themselves with the meat of Leviathan, as they boast of their good deeds.

Is there a God? Is He all merciful? Will Zirel ever find salvation? Or is creation a snake primeval crawling with evil? How can I tell? I'm still only a minor devil. Imps seldom get pro-

moted. Meanwhile generations come and go,
Zirel follows Zirel, in a myriad of reflections—
a myriad of mirrors.

Translated by Norbert Guterman

THE LITTLE
SHOEMAKERS

I

The Shoemakers and Their Family Tree

The family of the little shoemakers was famous
not only in Frampol but in the outlying district—in Yonev, Kreshev, Bilgoray, and even
in Zamoshoh. Abba Shuster, the founder of the
line, appeared in Frampol some time after
Chmielnitzki's pogroms. He brought himself a
plot of ground on the stubby hill behind the
butcher stalls, and there he built a house that
remained standing until just the other day. Not
that it was in such fine condition—the stone
foundation settled, the small windows warped,
and the shingled roof turned a moldy green and
was hung with swallows' nests. The door, moreover, sank into the ground; the banisters became bowlegged; and instead of stepping up
onto the threshold, one was obliged to step
down. All the same, it did survive the innumerable fires that devastated Frampol in the
early days. But the rafters were so rotten that
mushrooms grew on them, and when wood dust
was needed to staunch the blood of a circumcision, one had only to break off a piece of the
outer wall and rub it between one's fingers. The
roof, pitched so steeply that the chimneysweep

was unable to climb onto it to look after the chimney, was always catching fire from the sparks. It was only by the grace of God that the house was not overtaken by disaster.

The name of Abba Shuster is recorded, on parchment, in the annals of the Frampol Jewish community. It was his custom to make six pairs of shoes every year for distribution among widows and orphans; in recognition of his philanthropy the synagogue called him to the reading of the Torah under the honorific title, *Murenu,* meaning "our teacher."

His stone in the old cemetery had vanished, but the shoemakers knew a sign for the grave—nearby grew a hazelnut tree. According to the old wives, the tree sprang from Reb Abba's beard.

Reb Abba had five sons; they settled, all but one, in the neighboring towns; only Getzel remained in Frampol. He continued his father's charitable practice of making shoes for the poor, and he too was active in the gravediggers' brotherhood.

The annals go on to say that Getzel had a son, Godel, and that to Godel was born Treitel, and to Treitel, Gimpel. The shoemaker's art was handed down from one generation to the next. A principle was fast established in the family, requiring the eldest son to remain at home and succeed his father at the workbench.

The shoemakers resembled one another. They were all short, sandy-haired, and sound, honest

workmen. The people of Frampol believed that
Reb Abba, the head of the line, had learned
shoemaking from a master of the craft in Brod,
who divulged to him the secret of strengthening
leather and making it durable. In the cellar of
their house the little shoemakers kept a vat for
soaking hides. God knows what strange chemicals they added to the tanning fluid. They did
not disclose the formula to outsiders, and it was
handed on from father to son.

As it is not our business to deal with all the
generations of the little shoemakers, we will
confine ourselves to the last three. Reb Lippe
remained without heir till his old age, and it
was taken for a certainty that the line would
end with him. But when he was in his late sixties his wife died and he married an overripe
virgin, a milkmaid, who bore him six children.
The eldest son, Feivel, was quite well.to do. He
was prominent in community affairs, attended
all the important meetings, and for years served
as sexton of the tailors' synagogue. It was the
custom in this synagogue to select a new sexton
every Simchath Torah. The man so selected was
honored by having a pumpkin placed on his
head; the pumpkin was set with lighted candles,
and the lucky fellow was led about from house
to house and refreshed at each stop with wine
and strudel or honeycakes. However, Reb Feivel
happened to die on Simchath Torah, the day of
rejoicing over the Law, while dutifully making
these rounds; he fell flat in the market place,

and there was no reviving him. Because Feivel had been a notable philanthropist, the rabbi who conducted his services declared that the candles he had borne on his head would light his way to Paradise. The will found in his strongbox requested that when he was carried to the cemetery, a hammer, an awl, and a last should be laid on the black cloth over his coffin, in sign of the fact that he was a man of peaceful industry who never cheated his customers. His will was done.

Feivel's eldest son was called Abba, after the founder. Like the rest of his stock, he was short and thickset, with a broad yellow beard, and a high forehead lined with wrinkles, such as only rabbis and shoemakers have. His eyes were also yellow, and the over-all impression he created was that of a sulky hen. Nevertheless he was a clever workman, charitable like his forbears, and unequaled in Frampol as a man of his word. He would never make a promise unless he was sure he could fulfill it; when he was not sure he said: who knows, God willing, or maybe. Furthermore he was a man of some learning. Every day he read a chapter of the Torah in Yiddish translation and occupied his free time with chapbooks. Abba never missed a single sermon of the traveling preachers who came to town, and he was especially fond of the Biblical passages which were read in the synagogue during the winter months. When his wife, Pesha, read to him, of a Sabbath, from the Yiddish trans-

lation of the stories in the Book of Genesis, he
would imagine that he was Noah, and that his
sons were Shem, Ham, and Japheth. Or else he
would see himself in the image of Abraham,
Isaac, or Jacob. He often thought that if the
Almighty were to call on him to sacrifice his
eldest son, Gimpel, he would rise early in the
morning and carry out his commands without
delay. Certainly he would have left Poland and
the house of his birth and gone wandering over
the earth where God sent him. He knew the
story of Joseph and his brothers by heart, but
he never tired of reading it over again. He envied the ancients because the King of the Universe revealed Himself to them and performed
miracles for their sake, but consoled himself by
thinking that from him, Abba, to the Patri-
archs, there stretched an unbroken chain of
generations—as if he too were part of the Bible.
He sprang from Jacob's loins; he and his sons
were of the seed whose number had become like
the sand and the stars. He was living in exile
because the Jews of the Holy Land had sinned,
but he awaited the Redemption, and he would
be ready when the time came.

Abba was by far the best shoemaker in Frampol. His boots were always a perfect fit, never
too tight or too roomy. People who suffered from
chilblains, corns, or varicose veins were especially pleased with his work, claiming that his
shoes relieved them. He despised the new styles,
the gimcrack boots and slippers with fancy

heels and poorly stitched soles that fell apart with the first rain. His customers were respectable burghers of Frampol or peasants from the surrounding villages, and they deserved the best. He took their measurements with a knotted string, as in the old days. Most of the Frampol women wore wigs, but his wife, Pesha, covered her head with a bonnet as well. She bore him seven sons, and he named them after his forefathers—Gimpel, Getzel, Treitel, Godel, Feivel, Lippe, and Chananiah. They were all short and sandy-haired like their father. Abba predicted that he would turn them into shoemakers, and as a man of his word he let them look on at the workbench while they were still quite young, and at times taught them the old maxim—good work is never wasted.

He spent sixteen hours a day at the bench, a sack spread on his knees, gouging holes with the awl, sewing with a wire needle, tinting and polishing the leather or scraping it with a piece of glass; and while he worked he hummed snatches from the canticles of the Days of Awe. Usually the cat huddled nearby and watched the proceedings as though she were looking after him. Her mother and grandmother had caught mice, in their time, for the little shoemakers. Abba could look down the hill through the window and see the whole town and a considerable distance beyond, as far as the road to Bilgoray and the pine woods. He observed the groups of matrons who gathered every morning at the butcher stalls and the young men and idlers who went in and out of the courtyard of the synagogue; the girls going to the pump to draw water for tea, and the women hurrying at dusk to the ritual bath.

Evenings, when the sun was setting, the house would be pervaded by a dusky glow. Rays of light danced in the corners, flicked across the ceiling, and set Abba's beard gleaming with the color of spun gold. Pesha, Abba's wife, would be cooking *kasha* and soup in the kitchen, the children would be playing, neighboring women and girls would go in and out of the house. Abba would rise from his work, wash his hands, put on his long coat, and go off to the tailors' synagogue for evening prayers. He knew that the wide world was full of strange cities and distant lands, that Frampol was actually no bigger than a dot in a small prayer book; but it seemed to him that his little town was the navel of the universe and that his own house stood at the very center. He often thought that when the Messiah came to lead the Jews to the Land of Israel, he, Abba, would stay behind in Frampol, in his own house, on his own hill. On the Sabbath and on Holy Days would he step into a cloud and let himself be flown to Jerusalem.

II

Abba and His Seven Sons

Since Gimpel was the eldest, and therefore destined to succeed his father, he came foremost in Abba's concern. He sent him to the best Hebrew teachers and even hired a tutor who taught him the elements of Yiddish, Polish, Russian, and arithmetic. Abba himself led the boy down into the cellar and showed him the formula for adding chemicals and various kinds of bark to the tanning fluid. He revealed to him that in most cases the right foot is larger than the left, and that the source of all trouble in the fitting of shoes is usually to be found in the big toes. Then he taught Gimpel the principles for cutting soles and inner soles, snub-toed and pointed shoes, high heels and low; and for fitting customers with flat feet, bunions, hammer toes, and calluses.

On Fridays, when there was always a rush of work to get out, the older boys would leave *cheder* at ten in the morning and help their father in the shop. Pesha baked *chalah* and prepared their lunch. She would grasp the first loaf and carry it, hot from the oven, blowing on it all the while and tossing it from hand to hand, to show it to Abba, holding it up, front and back, till he nodded approval. Then she would return with a ladle and let him sample the fish soup, or ask him to taste a crumb of freshly baked cake. Pesha valued his judgment. When she went to buy cloth for herself or the children she brought home swatches for him to choose. Even before going to the butcher she asked his opinion—what should she get, breast or roast, flank or ribs? She consulted him not out of fear or because she had no mind of her own, but simply because she had learned that he always knew what he was talking about. Even when she was sure he was wrong, he would turn out to be right, after all. He never browbeat her, but merely cast a glance to let her know when she was being a fool. This was also the way he handled the children. A strap hung on the wall, but he seldom made use of it; he had his way by kindness. Even strangers respected him. The merchants sold him hides at a fair price and presented no objections when he asked for credit. His own customers trusted him and paid his prices without a murmur. He was always called sixth to the reading of the Torah in the tailors' synagogue—a considerable honor—and when he pledged or was assessed for money, it was never necessary to remind him. He paid up, without fail, right after the Sabbath. The town soon learned of his virtues, and though he was nothing but a plain shoemaker and, if the truth be told, something of an ignoramus, they treated him as they would a distinguished man.

When Gimpel turned thirteen, Abba girded the boys' loins in sackcloth and put him to work

at the bench. After Gimpel, Getzel, Treitel, Godel, and Feivel became apprentices. Though
they were his own sons and he supported them
out of his earnings, he nevertheless paid them
a wage. The two youngest boys, Lippe and
Chananiah, were still attending the elementary
cheder, but they too lent a hand at hammering
pegs. Abba and Pesha were proud of them. In
the morning the six workers trooped into the
kitchen for breakfast, washed their six pairs of
hands with the appropriate benediction, and
their six mouths chewed the roasted groats and
corn bread.

Abba loved to place his two youngest boys
one on each knee, and sing an old Frampol song
to them:

> *A mother had*
> *Ten little boys,*
> *Oh, Lord, ten little boys!*
>
> *The first one was Avremele,*
> *The second one was Berele,*
> *The third one was called Gimpele,*
> *The fourth one was called Dovid'l*
> *The fifth one was called Hershele....*

And all the boys came in on the chorus:

> *Oh, Lord, Hershele!*

Now that he had apprentices, Abba turned
out more work, and his income grew. Living

was cheap in Frampol, and since the peasants often made him a present of a measure of corn or a roll of butter, a sack of potatoes or a pot of honey, a hen or a goose, he was able to save some money on food. As their prosperity increased, Pesha began to talk of rebuilding the house. The rooms were too narrow, the ceiling was too low. The floor shook underfoot. Plaster was peeling off the walls, and all sorts of maggots and worms crawled through the woodwork. The lived in constant fear that the ceiling would fall on their heads. Even though they kept a cat, the place was infested with mice. Pesha insisted that they tear down this ruin and build a larger house.

Abba did not immediately say no. He told his wife he would think it over. But after doing so, he expressed the opinion that he would rather keep things as they were. First of all, he was afraid to tear down the house, because this might bring bad luck. Second, he feared the evil eye—people were grudging and envious enough. Third, he found it hard to part with the home in which his parents and grandparents, and the whole family, stretching back for generations, had lived and died. He knew every corner of the house, each crack and wrinkle. When one layer of paint peeled off the wall, another, of a different color, was exposed; and behind this layer, still another. The walls were like an album in which the fortunes of the family had been recorded. The attic was stuffed with heirlooms—tables and chairs, cobbler's benches and lasts, whetstones and knives, old clothes, pots, pans, bedding, salting boards, cradles. Sacks full of torn prayer books lay spilled on the floor.

Abba loved to climb up to the attic on a hot summer's day. Spiders spun great webs, and the sunlight, filtering in through cracks, fell upon the threads in rainbows. Everything lay under a thick coat of dust. When he listened attentively he would hear a whispering, a murmuring and soft scratching, as of some unseen creature engaged in endless activity, conversing in an unearthly tongue. He was sure that the souls of his forefathers kept watch over the house. In much the say way he loved the ground on which it stood. The weeds were as high as a man's head. There was a dense growth of hairy and brambly vegetation all about the place—the very leaves and twigs would catch hold of one's clothing as though with teeth and claws. Flies and midges swarmed in the air and the ground crawled with worms and snakes of all descriptions. Ants had raised their hills in this thicket; field mice had dug their holes. A pear tree grew in the midst of this wilderness; every year, at the time of the Feast of the Tabernacle, it yielded small fruit with the taste and hardness of wood. Birds and bees flew over this jungle, great big golden-bellied flies. Toadstools sprang up after each rain. The ground was unkept, but an unseen hand guarded its fertility.

When Abba stood here looking up at the summer sky, losing himself in contemplation of the clouds, shaped like sailboats, flocks of sheep, brooms, and elephant herds, he felt the presence of God, His providence and His mercy. He could virtually see the Almighty seated on His throne of glory, the earth serving Him as a footstool. Satan was vanquished; the angels sang hymns. The Book of Memory in which were recorded all the deeds of men lay open. From time to time, at sunset, it even seemed to Abba that he saw the river of fire in the nether world. Flames leaped up from the burning coals; a wave of fire rose, flooding the shores. When he listened closely he was sure he heard the muffled cries of sinners and the derisive laughter of the evil host.

No, this was good enough for Abba Shuster. There was nothing to change. Let everything stand as it had stood for ages, until he lived out his allotted time and was buried in the cemetery among his ancestors, who had shod the sacred community and whose good name was preserved not only in Frampol but in the surrounding district.

III

Gimpel Emigrates to America

Therefore the proverb says: Man proposes, God disposes.

One day while Abba was working on a boot, his eldest son, Gimpel, came into the shop. His freckled face was heated, his sandy hair disheveled under the skullcap. Instead of taking his place at the bench, he stopped at his father's side, regarded him hesitantly, and at last said, "Father, I must tell you something."

"Well, I'm not stopping you," replied Abba.

"Father," he cried, "I'm going to America."

Abba dropped his work. This was the last thing he expected to hear, and up went his eyebrows.

"What happened? Did you rob someone? Did you get into a fight?"

"No, Father."

"Then why are you running away?"

"There's no future for me in Frampol."

"Why not? You know a trade. God willing, you'll marry some day. You have everything to look forward to."

"I'm sick of small towns; I'm sick of the people. This is nothing but a stinking swamp."

"When they get around to draining it," said Abba, "there won't be any more swamp."

"No, Father, that's not what I mean."

"Then what do you mean?" cried Abba angrily. "Speak up!"

The boy spoke up, but Abba couldn't understand a word of it. He laid into synagogue and state with such venom, Abba could only imagine that the poor soul was possessed: the Hebrew teachers beat the children; the women

empty their slop pails right outside the door;
the shopkeepers loiter in the streets; there are
no toilets anywhere, and the public relieves itself as it pleases, behind the bathhouse or out
in the open, encouraging epidemics and plagues.
He made fun of Ezreal the Healer and of Mecheles the Marriage Broker, nor did he spare the
rabbinical court and the bath attendant, the
washerwoman and the overseer of the poorhouse, the professions and the benevolent so-
cieties.

At first Abba was afraid that the boy had lost
his mind, but the longer he continued his ha-
rangue, the clearer it became that he had
strayed from the path of righteousness. Jacob
Reifman, the atheist, used to hold forth in Shebreshin, not far from Frampol. A pupil of his,
a detractor of Israel, was in the habit of visiting
an aunt in Frampol and had gathered quite a
following among the good-for-nothings. It had
never occurred to Abba that his Gimpel might
fall in with this gang.

"What do you say, Father?" asked Gimpel.

Abba thought it over. He knew that there
was no use arguing with Gimpel, and he remembered the proverb: A rotten apple spoils
the barrel. "Well," he replied, "what can I do?
If you want to go, go. I won't stop you."

And he resumed his work.

But Pesha did not give in so easily. She
begged Gimpel not to go so far away; she wept
and implored him not to bring shame on the

family. She even ran to the cemetery, to the graves of her forefathers, to seek the intercession of the dead. But she was finally convinced that Abba was right: it was no use arguing. Gimpel's face had turned hard as leather, and a mean light showed in his yellow eyes. He had become a stranger in his own home. He spent that night out with friends, and returned in the morning to pack his prayer shawl and phylacteries, a few shirts, a blanket, and some hardboiled eggs—and he was all set to go. He had saved enough money for passage. When his mother saw that it was settled, she urged him to take at least a jar of preserves, a bottle of cherry juice, bedding, pillows. But Gimpel refused. He was going to steal over the border into Germany, and he stood a better chance if he traveled light. In short, he kissed his mother, said good-by to his brothers and friends, and off he went. Abba, not wanting to part with his son in anger, took him in the wagon to the station at Reivetz. The train arrived in the middle of the night with a hissing and whistling, a racket and din. Abba took the headlights of the locomotive for the eyes of a hideous devil, and shied away from the funnels with their columns of sparks and smoke and their clouds of steam. The blinding lights only intensified the darkness. Gimpel ran around with his baggage like a madman, and his father ran after him. At the last moment the boy kissed his father's hand, and Abba called after him, into the darkness, "Good luck! Don't forsake your religion!"

The train pulled out, leaving a smell of smoke in Abba's nostrils and a ringing in his ears. The earth trembled under his feet. As though the boy had been dragged off by demons! When he returned home and Pesha fell on him, weeping, he said to her, "The Lord gave and the Lord has taken away...."

Months passed without word from Gimpel. Abba knew that this was the way with young men when they leave home—they forget their dearest ones. As the proverb says: Out of sight, out of mind. He doubted that he would ever hear from him, but one day a letter came from America. Abba recognized his son's handwriting. Gimpel wrote that he crossed the border safely, that he saw many strange cities and spent four weeks on board ship, living on potatoes and herring because he did not want to touch improper food. The ocean was very deep and the waves as high as the sky. He saw flying fish but no mermaids or mermen, and he did not hear them singing. New York is a big city, the houses reach into the clouds. The trains go over the roofs. The gentiles speak English. No one walks with his eyes on the ground, everybody holds his head high. He met a lot of his countrymen in New York; they all wear short coats. He too. The trade he learned at home has come in very handy. He is *all right*; he is earning a living. He will write again, a long letter. He kisses his father and mother and his brothers, and sends regards to his friends.

A friendly letter after all.

In his second letter Gimpel announced that he had fallen in love with a girl and bought her a diamond ring. Her name is Bessie; she comes from Rumania; and she works *at dresses*. Abba put on his spectacles with the brass frames and spent a long time puzzling this out. Where did the boy learn so many English words? The third letter stated that he was married and that *a reverend* had performed the service. He enclosed a snapshot of himself and wife.

Abba could not believe it. His son was wearing a gentleman's coat and a high hat. The bride was dressed like a countess in a white dress, with train and veil; she held a bouquet of flowers in her hand. Pesha took one look at the snapshot and began to cry. Gimpel's brothers gaped. Neighbors came running, and friends from all over town: they could have sworn that Gimpel had been spirited away by magic to a land of gold, where he had taken a princess to wife—just as in the storybooks the pack merchants brought to town.

To make a long story short, Gimpel induced Getzel to come to America, and Getzel brought over Treitel; Godel followed Treitel, and Feivel, Godel; and then all five brothers brought the young Lippe and Chananiah across. Pesha lived only for the mail. She fastened a charity box to the doorpost, and whenever a letter came she dropped a coin through the slot. Abba worked all alone. He no longer needed apprentices because he now had few expenses and could afford to earn less; in fact, he could have given up work altogether, as his sons sent him money from abroad. Nevertheless he rose at his usual early hour and remained at the bench until late in the evening. His hammer sounded away, joined by the cricket on the hearth, the mouse in its hole, the shingles crackling on the roof. But his mind reeled. For generations the little shoemakers had lived in Frampol. Suddenly the birds had flown the coop. Was this a punishment, a judgment, on him? Did it make sense?

Abba bored a hole, stuck in a peg, and murmured, "So—you, Abba know what you're doing and God does not? Shame on you, fool! His will be done. Amen!"

IV

The Sack of Frampol

Almost forty years went by. Pesha had long since died of cholera, during the Austrian occupation. And Abba's sons had grown rich in America. They wrote every week, begging him to come and join them, but he remained in Frampol, in the same old house on the stubby hill. His own grave lay ready, next to Pesha's, among the little shoemakers; the stone had already been raised; only the date was missing. Abba put up a bench by the side of her grave, and on the eve of Rosh Hashonoh or during fasts, he went there to pray and read Lamentations. He loved it in the cemetery. The sky was so much clearer and loftier than in town, and a great, meaningful silence rose from the consecrated ground and the old gravestone overgrown with moss. He loved to sit and look at the tall white birches, which trembled even when no breeze blew, and at the crows balancing in the branches, like black fruit. Before she died Pesha made him promise that he would not remarry and that he would come regularly to her grave with news of the children. He kept his promise. He would stretch out alongside the mound and whisper into her ear, as if she were still alive, "Gimpel has another grandchild. Getzel's youngest daughter is engaged, thank God...."

The house on the hill was nearly in ruins. The beams had rotted away, and the roof had to be supported by stone posts. Two of the three windows were boarded over because it was no longer possible to fit glass to the frames. The floor was all but gone, and the bare ground lay exposed to the feet. The pear tree in the garden had withered; the trunk and branches were covered with scales. The garden itself was now overgrown with poisonous berries and grapes, and there was a profusion of the burrs that children throw about on Tishe b'Av. People swore they saw strange fires burning there at night, and claimed that the attic was full of bats which fly into girls' hair. Be that as it may, an owl certainly did hoot somewhere near the house. The neighbors repeatedly warned Abba to move out of this ruin before it was too late—the least wind might knock it over. They pleaded with him to give up working—his sons were showering him with money. But Abba stubbornly rose at dawn and continued at the shoemaker's bench. Although yellow hair does not readily change color, Abba's beard had turned completely white, and the white, staining, had turned yellow again. His brows had sprouted like brushes and hid his eyes, and his high forehead was like a piece of yellow parchment. But he had not lost his touch. He could still turn out a stout shoe with a broad heel, even if it did take a little longer. He bored holes with awl, stitched with the needle, hammered his pegs, and in a hoarse voice sang the old shoemaker's song:

> "A mother bought a billy goat,
> The shochet killed the billy goat,
> Oh, Lord, the billy goat!
> Avremele took its ears,
> Berele took its lung,
> Gimpele took the gullet,
> And Dovid'l took the tongue,
> Hershele took the neck. . . ."

As there was no one to join him, he now sang the chorus alone:

> "Oh, Lord, the billy goat!"

His friends urged him to hire a servant, but he would not take a strange woman into the house. Occasionally one of the neighbor women came in to sweep and dust, but even this was too much for him. He got used to being alone. He learned to cook for himself and would prepare soup on the tripod, and on Fridays even put up the pudding for the Sabbath. Best of all, he liked to sit alone at the bench and follow the course of his thoughts, which had become more and more tangled with the years. Day and night he carried on conversations with himself. One voice asked questions, the other answered. Clever words came to his mind, sharp, timely expressions full of the wisdom of age, as though his grandfathers had come to life again and were conducting their endless disputations inside his head on matters pertaining to this world and the next. All his thoughts ran on one theme: What is life and what is death, what is time that goes on without stopping, and how far away is America? His eyes would close; the hammer would fall out of his hand; but he would still hear the cobbler's characteristic rapping— a soft tap, a louder one, and a third, louder still—as if a ghost sat at his side, mending unseen shoes. When one of the neighbors asked him why he did not go to join his sons, he would point to the heap on the bench and say, "*Nu*, and the shoes? Who will mend them?"

Years passed, and he had no idea how or where they vanished. Traveling preachers passed through Frampol with disturbing news of the outside world. In the tailors' synagogue, which

Abba still attended, the young men spoke of war and anti-Semitic decrees, of Jews flocking to Palestine. Peasants who had been Abba's customers for years suddenly deserted him and took their trade to Polish shoemakers. And one day the old man heard that a new world war was imminent. Hitler—may his name vanish!—had raised his legions of barbarians and was threatening to grab up Poland. This scourge of Israel had expelled the Jews from Germany, as in the days of Spain. The old man thought of the Messiah and became terribly excited. Who knows? Perhaps this was the battle of Gog and Magog? Maybe the Messiah really was coming and the dead would rise again! He saw the graves opening and the little shoemakers stepping forth—Abba, Getzel, Treitel, Gimpel, his grandfather, his own father. He called them all into his house and set out brandy and cakes. His wife, Pesha, was ashamed to find the house in such condition, but "Never mind," he assured her, "we'll get someone to sweep up. As long as we're all together!" Suddenly a cloud appears, envelops the town of Frampol—synagogue, House of Study, ritual bath, all the Jewish homes, his own among them—and carries the whole settlement off to the Holy Land. Imagine his amazement when he encounters his sons from America. They fall at his feet, crying, "Forgive us, Father!"

When Abba pictured this event his hammer quickened in tempo. He saw the little shoemakers dress for the Sabbath in silks and satins, in flowing robes with broad sashes, and go forth rejoicing in Jerusalem. They pray in the Temple of Solomon, drink the wine of Paradise, and eat of the mighty steer and Leviathan. The ancient Jochanan the Shoemaker, renown for his piety and wisdom, greets the family and engages them in a discussion of Torah and shoemaking. Sabbath over, the whole clan returns to Frampol, which has become part of the Land of Israel, and re-enters the old home. Even though the house is as small as ever, it has miraculously grown roomy enough, like the hide of a deer, as it is written in the Book. They all work at one bench, Abbas, Gimpels, Getzels, Godels, the Treitels and the Lippes, sewing golden sandals for the daughters of Zion and lordly boots for the sons. The Messiah himself calls on the little shoemakers and has them take his measure for a pair of silken slippers.

One morning, while Abba was wandering among his thoughts, he heard a tremendous crash. The old man shook in his bones: the blast of the Messiah's trumpet! He dropped the boot he had been working on and ran out in ecstasy. But it was not Elijah the Prophet proclaiming the Messiah. Nazi planes were bombing Frampol. Panic spread through the town. A bomb fell near the synagogue, so loud that Abba felt his brain shudder in his skull. Hell opened before him. There was a blaze of lightning, followed by a blast that illuminated all of Frampol. A black cloud rose over the courtyard of the synagogue. Flocks of birds flapped about in the sky. The forest was burning. Looking down from his hill, Abba saw the orchards under great columns of smoke. The apple trees were blossoming and burning. Several men who stood near him threw themselves down on the ground and shouted to him to do the same. He did not hear them; they were moving their lips in dumbshow. Shaking with fright, his knees knocking together, he reentered the house and packed a sack with his prayer shawl and phylacteries, a shirt, his shoemaker's tools, and the paper money he had put away in the straw mattress. Then he took up a stick, kissed the *mezzuzah*, and walked out the door. It was a miracle that he was not killed; the house caught fire the moment he left. The roof swung out like a lid, uncovering the attic with its treasures. The walls collapsed. Abba turned about and saw the shelf of sacred books go up in flames. The blackened pages turned in the air, glowing with fiery letters like the Torah given to the Jews on Mount Sinai.

V

Across the Ocean

From that day on, Abba's life was transformed beyond recognition—it was like a story he had read in the Bible, a fantastic tale heard from the lips of a visiting preacher. He had abandoned the house of his forefathers and the place of his birth and, staff in hand, gone wandering into the world like the Patriarch Abraham. The havoc in Frampol and the surrounding villages brought Sodom and Gomorrah to mind, burning like a fiery furnace. He spent his nights in the cemetery together with the other Jews, lying with his head on a gravestone—he too, as Jacob did at Beth-El, on the way from Beer Sheba to Haran.

On Rosh Hashonoh the Frampol Jews held services in the forest, with Abba leading the most solemn prayer of the Eighteen Benedictions because he was the only one with a prayer shawl. He stood under a pine tree, which served as an altar, and in a hoarse voice intoned the litany of the Days of Awe. A cuckoo and a woodpecker accompanied him, and all the birds roundabout twittered, whistled, and screeched. Late summer gossamers wafted through the air and trailed onto Abba's beard. From time to time a lowing sounded through the forest, like a blast on the ram's horn. As the Day of Atonement drew near, the Jews of Frampol rose at midnight to say the prayer for forgiveness, reciting it in fragments, whatever they could remember. The horses in the surrounding pastures whinnied and neighed, frogs croaked in the cool night. Distant gunfire sounded intermittently; the clouds shone red. Meteors fell; flashes of lightning played across the sky. Half-starved little children, exhausted from crying, took sick and died in their mothers' arms. There were many burials in the open fields. A woman gave birth.

Abba felt he had become his own great-great-grandfather, who had fled Chmielnitzki's pogroms, and whose name is recorded in the annals of Frampol. He was ready to offer himself in Sanctification of the Name. He dreamed of priests and Inquisitions, and when the wind blew among the branches he heard martyred Jews crying out, "Hear, O Israel, the Lord our God, the Lord is One!"

Fortunately Abba was able to help a good many Jews with his money and shoemaker's tools. With the money they hired wagons and fled south, toward Rumania; but often they had to walk long distances, and their shoes gave out. Abba would stop under a tree and take up his tools. With God's help, they surmounted danger and crossed the Rumanian frontier at night. The next morning, the day before Yom Kippur, an old widow took Abba into her house. A telegram was sent to Abba's sons in America, informing them that their father was safe.

You may be sure that Abba's sons moved heaven and earth to rescue the old man. When they learned of his whereabouts they ran to Washington and with great difficulty obtained a visa for him; then they wired a sum of money to the consul in Bucharest, begging him to help their father. The consul sent a courier to Abba, and he was put on the train to Bucharest. There he was held a week, then transferred to an Italian seaport, where he was shorn and deloused and had his clothes steamed. He was put on board the last ship for the United States.

It was a long and severe journey. The train from Rumania to Italy dragged on, uphill and down, for thirty-six hours. He was given food, but for fear of touching anything ritually unclean he ate nothing at all. His phylacteries and prayer shawl got lost, and with them he lost all track of time and could no longer distinguish between Sabbath and weekdays. Apparently he was the only Jewish passenger on board. There was a man on the ship who spoke German, but Abba could not understand him.

It was a stormy crossing. Abba spent almost the whole time lying down, and frequently vomited gall, though he took nothing but dry crusts and water. He would doze off and wake to the sound of the engines throbbing day and night, to the long, threatening signal blasts, which reeked of fire and brimstone. The door of his cabin was constantly slamming to and fro, as though an imp were swinging on it. The glassware in the cupboard trembled and danced; the walls shook; the deck rocked like a cradle.

During the day Abba kept watch at the porthole over his bunk. The ship would leap up as if mounting the sky, and the torn sky would fall as though the world were returning to original chaos. Then the ship would plunge back into

the ocean, and once again the firmament would
be divided from the waters, as in the Book of
Genesis. The waves were a sulphurous yellow
and black. Now they would saw-tooth out to the
horizon like a mountain range, reminding Abba
of the Psalmist's words: "The mountains skipped
like rams, the little hills like lambs." Then they
would come heaving back, as in the miraculous
Parting of the Waters. Abba had little learning,
but Biblical references ran through his mind,
and he saw himself as the prophet Jonah, who
fled before God. He too lay in the belly of a
whale and, like Jonah, prayed to God for deliv-
erance. Then it would seem to him that this was
not ocean but limitless desert, crawling with
serpents, monsters, and dragons, as it is written
in Deuteronomy. He hardly slept a wink at
night. When he got up to relieve himself, he
would feel faint and lose his balance. With great
difficulty he would regain his feet and, his
knees buckling under, go wandering, lost, down
the narrow, winding corridor, groaning and
calling for help until a sailor led him back to
the cabin. Whenever this happened he was sure
that he was dying. He would not even receive
decent Jewish burial, but be dumped in the
ocean. And he made his confession, beating his
knotty fist on his chest and exclaiming, "Forgive me, Father!"

Just as he was unable to remember when he
began his voyage, so he was unaware when it
came to an end. The ship had already been made

fast to the dock in New York harbor, but Abba
hadn't the vaguest notion of this. He saw huge
buildings and towers, but mistook them for the
pyramids of Egypt. A tall man in a white hat
came into the cabin and shouted something at
him, but he remained motionless. At last they
helped him dress and led him out on deck, where
his sons and daughters-in-law and grandchildren were waiting. Abba was bewildered; a
crowd of Polish landowners, counts and count-
esses, gentile boys and girls, leaped at him,
hugged him, and kissed him, crying out in a
strange language, which was both Yiddish and
not Yiddish. They half led, half carried him
away, and placed him in a car. Other cars arrived, packed with Abba's kinfolk, and they set
out, speeding like shot arrows over bridges, rivers, and roofs. Buildings rose up and receded,
as if by magic, some of the buildings touching
the sky. Whole cities lay spread out before him;
Abba thought of Pithom and Rameses. The car
sped so fast, it seemed to him the people in the
streets were moving backward. The air was full
of thunder and lightning; a banging and trum-
peting, it was a wedding and a conflagration at
once. The nations had gone wild, a heathen fes-
tival . . .

His sons were crowding around him. He saw
them as in a fog and did not know them. Short
men with white hair. They shouted, as if he
were deaf.

"I'm Gimpel!"

"Getzel!"

"Feivel!"

The old man closed his eyes and made no answer. Their voices ran together; everything was turning pell-mell, topsy-turvy. Suddenly he thought of Jacob arriving in Egypt, where he was met by Pharaoh's chariots. He felt he had lived through the same experience in a previous incarnation. His beard began to tremble; a hoarse sob rose from his chest. A forgotten passage from the Bible stuck in his gullet.

Blindly he embraced one of his sons and sobbed out, "Is this you? Alive?"

He had meant to say: "Now let me die, since I have seen thy face, because thou art yet alive."

VI
The American Heritage

Abba's sons lived on the outskirts of a town in New Jersey. Their seven homes, surrounded by gardens, stood on the shore of a lake. Every day they drove to the shoe factory, owned by Gimpel, but on the day of Abba's arrival they took a holiday and prepared a feast in his honor. It was to be held in Gimpel's house, in full compliance with the dietary laws. Gimpel's wife, Bessie, whose father had been a Hebrew teacher in the old country, remembered all the rituals and observed them carefully, going so far as to cover her head with a kerchief. Her sisters-in-law did the same, and Abba's sons put on the skullcaps they had once worn during Holy Days. The grandchildren and great-grandchildren, who did not know a word of Yiddish, actually learned a few phrases. They had heard the legends of Frampol and the little shoemakers and the first Abba of the family line. Even the gentiles in the neighborhood were fairly well acquainted with this history. In the ads Gimpel published in the papers, he had proudly disclosed that his family belonged to the shoemaking aristocracy:

> Our experience dates back three hundred years to the Polish city of Brod, where our ancestor, Abba, learned the craft from a local master. The community of Frampol, in which our family worked at its trade for fifteen generations, bestowed on him the title of Master in recognition of his charitable services. This sense of public responsibility has always gone hand in hand with our devotion to the highest principles of the craft and our strict policy of honest dealing with our customers.

The day Abba arrived, the papers in Elizabeth carried a notice to the effect that the seven brothers of the famous shoe company were welcoming their father from Poland. Gimpel received a mass of congratulatory telegrams from rival manufacturers, relatives, and friends.

It was an extraordinary feast. Three tables

were spread in Gimpel's dining-room; one for the old man, his sons, and daughters-in-law, another for the grandchildren, and the third for the great-grandchildren. Although it was broad daylight, the tables were set with candles—red, blue, yellow, green—and their flames were reflected from the dishes and silverware, the crystal glasses and the wine cups, the decanters reminiscent of the Passover Seder. There was an abundance of flowers in every available corner. To be sure, the daughters-in-law would have preferred to see Abba properly dressed for the occasion, but Gimpel put his foot down, and Abba was allowed to spend his first day in the familiar long coat, Frampol style. Even so, Gimpel hired a photographer to take pictures of the banquet—for publication in the newspapers— and invited a rabbi and a cantor to the feast to honor the old man with traditional song.

Abba sat in an armchair at the head of the table. Gimpel and Getzel brought in a bowl and poured water over his hands for the benediction before eating. The food was served on silver trays, carried by colored women. All sorts of fruit juices and salads were set before the old man, sweet brandies, cognac, caviar. But Pharaoh, Joseph, Potiphar's wife, the Land of Goshen, the chief baker, and the chief butler spun round and round in his head. His hands trembled so that he was unable to feed himself, and Gimpel had to help him. No matter how often his sons spoke to him, he still could not tell them apart. Whenever the phone rang he jumped—the Nazis were bombing Frampol. The entire house was whirling round and round like a carousel; the tables were standing on the ceiling and everyone sat upside down. His face was sickly pale in the light of the candles and the electric bulbs. He fell asleep soon after the soup course, while the chicken was being served. Quickly they led him to the bedroom, undressed him, and called a doctor.

He spent several weeks in bed, in and out of consciousness, fitfully dozing as in a fever. He even lacked the strength to say his prayers. There was a nurse at his bedside day and night. Eventually he recovered enough to take a few steps outdoors, in front of the house, but his senses remained disordered. He would walk into clothes closets, lock himself into the bathroom and forget how to come out; the doorbell and the radio frightened him; and he suffered constant anxiety because of the cars that raced past the house. One day Gimpel brought him to a synagogue ten miles away, but even here he was bewildered. The sexton was clean-shaven; the candelabra held electric lights; there was no courtyard, no faucet for washing one's hands, no stove to stand around. The cantor, instead of singing like a cantor should, babbled and croaked. The congregation wore tiny little prayer shawls, like scarves around their necks. Abba was sure he had been hauled into church to be converted. . . .

When spring came and he was no better, the daughters-in-law began to hint that it wouldn't be such a bad idea to put him in a home. But something unforeseen took place. One day, as he happened to open a closet, he noticed a sack lying on the floor which seemed somehow familiar. He looked again and recognized his shoemaker's equipment from Frampol: last, hammer and nails, his knife and pliers, the file and the awl, even a broken-down shoe. Abba felt a tremor of excitement; he could hardly believe his eyes. He sat down on a footstool and began to poke about with fingers grown clumsy and stale. When Bessie came in and found him playing with a dirty old shoe, she burst out laughing.

"What are you doing, Father? Be careful, you'll cut yourself, God forbid!"

That day Abba did not lie in bed dozing. He worked busily till evening and even ate his usual piece of chicken with greater appetite. He smiled at the grandchildren when they came in to see what he was doing. The next morning, when Gimpel told his brothers how their father had returned to his old habits, they laughed and thought nothing more of it—but the activity soon proved to be the old man's salvation. He kept at it day after day without tiring, hunting up old shoes in the clothes closets and begging his sons to supply him with leather and tools. When they gave in, he mended every last pair of shoes in the house—man, woman, and child's.

After the Passover holidays the brothers got together and decided to build a little hut in the yard. They furnished it with a cobbler's bench, a stock of leather soles and hides, nails, dyes, brushes—everything even remotely useful in the craft.

Abba took on new life. His daughters-in-law cried, he looked fifteen years younger. As in the Frampol days, he now rose at dawn, said his prayers, and got right to work. Once again he used a knotted string as a measuring tape. The first pair of shoes, which he made for Bessie, became the talk of the neighborhood. She had always complained of her feet, but this pair, she insisted, were the most comfortable shoes she had ever worn. The other girls soon followed her example and also had themselves fitted. Then came the grandchildren. Even some of the gentile neighbors came to Abba when they heard that in sheer joy of the work he was turning out custom-made shoes. He had to communicate with them, for the most part, in gestures, but they got along very well. As for the younger grandchildren and the great-grandchildren, they had long been in the habit of standing at the door to watch him work. Now he was earning money, and he plied them with candies and toys. He even whittled a stylus and began to instruct them in the elements of Hebrew and piety.

One Sunday, Gimpel came into the workshop and, no more than half in earnest, rolled up his sleeves and joined Abba at the bench. The other brothers were not to be outdone, and on the following Sunday eight work stools were set up in the hut. Abba's sons spread sackcloth aprons on their knees and went to work, cutting soles and shaping heels, boring holes and hammering pegs, as in the good old days. The women stood outside, laughing, but they took pride in their men, and the children were fascinated. The sun streamed in through the windows, and motes of dust danced in the light. In the high spring sky, lofting over the grass and the water, floated clouds in the form of brooms, sailboats, flocks of sheep, herds of elephants. Birds sang; flies buzzed; butterflies fluttered about.

Abba raised his dense eyebrows, and his sad eyes looked around at his heirs, the seven shoemakers: Gimpel, Getzel, Treitel, Godel, Feivel, Lippe, and Chananiah. Their hair was white, though yellow streaks remained. No, praise God, they had not become idolaters in Egypt. They had not forgotten their heritage, nor had they lost themselves among the unworthy. The old man rattled and bumbled deep in his chest, and suddenly began to sing in a stifled, hoarse voice:

> *"A mother had*
> *Ten little boys,*
> *Oh, Lord, ten little boys!*

The sixth one was called Velvele,
The seventh one was Zeinvele,
The eighth one was called Chenele,
The ninth one was called Tevele,
The tenth one was called Judele ..."

And Abba's sons came in on the chorus:

"Oh, Lord, Judele!"

Translated by Isaac Rosenfeld

JOY

I

Rabbi Bainish of Komarov, having buried Bunem, his third son, stopped praying for his ailing children. Only one son and two daughters remained, and all of them spat blood. His wife, frequently breaking into the solitude of his study would scream, "Why are you so silent? Why don't you move heaven and earth?" With clenched fists raised, she would wail, "What good are your knowledge, your prayers, the merits of your ancestors, your prolonged fasts? What does He have against you—our Father in Heaven? Why must all His anger be directed against you?" In her despair she once snatched a sacred book and threw it on the floor. Silently, Rabbi Bainish picked it up. His invariable answer was, "Leave me alone!"

Though he was not yet fifty, the rabbi's beard, so thin that the hairs could be numbered, had turned white as the beard of an old man. His tall body stooped. His stern black eyes looked past everyone. No longer did he comment on the Torah nor preside over meals. For weeks now he had not appeared at the House of Study. Though his followers came from other towns to

visit him, they had to return without being allowed even a greeting. Behind his bolted door
he sat, silent; it was a pregnant silence. The
crowd, his "bread and butter" Hassidim, gradually dispersed among other rabbis. Only his
intimate circle, the old Hassidim, the wise ones,
stayed. When Rebecca, his youngest daughter,
died, the rabbi did not even follow her hearse.
He gave orders to his sexton, Avigdor, to close
the shutters, and they remained closed. Through
a heart-shaped aperture in the shutters, came
the meager light whereby the rabbi looked
through books. He no longer recited the texts
out loud; he merely thumbed the pages, opening
a book at one place and then at another, and
with one eye closed, stared vacantly beyond the
pages and the walls. Dipping his pen in the
inkwell, he would move a sheet of paper close
to him, but he could not write. He would fill a
pipe, but it remained unlit. There was no indication that he had touched the breakfast and
supper that had been brought to his study.
Weeks, months, went by like this.

One summer day the rabbi appeared at the
House of Study. Several boys and young men
were studying there, while a couple of old men,
hangers-on, were meditating. Since their rabbi
had been absent for so long, all of them were
frightened at the sight of him. Taking a step in
one direction, and then a step back, the rabbi
asked, "Where is Abraham Moshe of Borisov?"

"At the inn," said a young man who had not
yet been struck dumb.

"Would you ask him to come to me, please?"

"I will, Rabbi."

The young man left immediately for the inn. Walking to the bookshelves, the rabbi drew out a book at random, glanced at a page, and then replaced the book. In his unbuttoned robe, his long fringed garment, his short trousers, white stockings, with hat pushed back on his head, his earlocks unkempt, his eyebrows contracted, he stood there. The House of Study was so still that water could be heard dripping in the basin, and flies humming around the candlesticks. The grandfather clock, with its long chains and pomegranates on the dial, creaked and struck three. Through the open windows peeped the fruit trees in the orchard; one heard the chirping of birds. In the slanting pillars of dust, tiny particles vibrated, no longer matter, and not yet spirit, reflecting rainbow hues. The rabbi beckoned to a boy who had only recently left the Hebrew school and had begun to read the Talmud on his own.

"What's your name, eh?"

"Moshe."

"What are you studying?"

"The first treatise."

"What chapter?"

"Shur Shenagah ath haparah."

"How do you translate that?"

"A bull gored a cow."

The rabbi stamped his slippered foot. "Why did the bull gore the cow? What had the cow done to him?"

"A bull does not reason."

"But He who created the bull can reason."

The boy did not know the answer to that one. The rabbi pinched his cheek.

"Well, go study," he said, returning to his room.

Reb Abraham Moshe came to him shortly afterwards. He was a small, youthful-faced man, with white beard and earlocks, wearing a floor length robe, a thick, moss-green sash, and carrying a long pipe that reached to his knees. Over his skull cap he wore a high cap. His eccentricities were well known. He would recite the morning prayer in the afternoon, and the afternoon prayer long after others had returned from the evening service. He chanted psalms at Purim, and during the Kol Nidre prayer, he slept. On Passover eve when everyone celebrated at the Passover feast, he would study a Commentary of the Talmudic Treatises on Damages and Compensations. It was rumored that once, at the tavern, he had won a game of chess from a general, and that the general had rewarded him with a license to sell brandy. His wife ran the business; he himself, spent more time at Komarov than at home. He would say that living at Komarov was like standing at the foot of Mount Sinai; the air itself purified one. In a more jocular mood, he would comment that there was no need to study at Komarov; it was sufficient to loiter on a bench in the House of Study and inhale the Torah as

one breathed. The Hassidim knew that the
rabbi held Reb Abraham Moshe in the highest
esteem, discussed esoteric doctrine with him,
and asked his advice. Reb Abraham Moshe was
always seated at the head of the table. Nevertheless, each time he visited the rabbi, he
spruced up like a young man. He would wash
his hands, button his caftan, curl his earlocks,
and comb his beard. He would enter with rev-
erence, as one enters the house of a saint.

The rabbi had not sent for him since Rebecca's death; this in itself was an indication
of the depth of the rabbi's grief. Reb Abraham
Moshe did not shuffle now, as customarily, but
walked briskly, almost running. When he had
reached the rabbi's door he halted for a moment,
touched his cap, his chest, wiped his brow with
his handkerchief, and then walked in minc-
ingly. The rabbi, having opened one of the shutters, sat smoking his pipe in the grandfather's
chair with the ivory armrests. A half-full glass
of tea stood on the table, a roll beside it. Apparently, the rabbi had recovered.

"Rabbi, I'm here," said Reb Abraham Moshe.

"So I see. Be seated."

"Thank you."

The rabbi remained silent a while. Placing
his narrow hand on the table edge, he stared at
the white nails of his long fingers. Then he said,
"Abraham Moshe, it's bad."

"What's bad?"

"Abraham Moshe, it's worse than you think."

"What could be worse?" asked Abraham Moshe, ironically.

"Abraham Moshe, the atheists are right. There is no justice, no Judge."

Reb Abraham Moshe was accustomed to the rabbi's harsh words. At Komarov, even the Lord of the Universe would not be spared. But to be rebellious is one thing; to deny God, another. Reb Abraham Moshe turned pale. His knees shook.

"Then who rules the world, Rabbi?"

"It's not ruled."

"Who then?"

"A total lie!"

"Come, come..."

"A heap of dung..."

"Where did the dung come from?"

"In the beginning was the dung."

Reb Abraham Moshe froze. He wanted to speak, but his arguments caught in his throat. Well, it's his grief that talks, he thought. Nevertheless, he marvelled. If Job could endure it, so should the rabbi.

"What should we do, then, Rabbi?" Reb Abraham Moshe asked hoarsely.

"We should worship idols."

To keep from falling, Reb Abraham Moshe gripped the table edge.

"What idols?" he asked. Everything inside him seemed to tighten.

The rabbi laughed briefly. "Don't be frightened; I won't send you to the priest. If the athe-

ists are right, what's the difference between
Terah and Abraham? Each served a different
idol. Terah, who was simpleminded, invented
a clay god. Abraham invented a Creator. It is
what one invents that matters. Even a lie must
have some truth in it."

"You are merely being facetious," Reb Abraham Moshe stammered. His palate felt dry, his
throat contracted.

"Well, stop trembling! Sit down!"

Reb Abraham Moshe sat down. The rabbi
rose from his seat, walked to the window, and
stood there a long time, staring into space. Then
he walked to the book cabinet. The cabinet,
which smelled of wine and snuffed-out valedic-
tory candles, contained a spice-box, and citron
box, and a Chanukah candelabra. The rabbi,
taking out a Zohar, opened it at random, stared
at the page, nodded, and then, smacking his
lips, exclaimed, "A nice invention, very nice!"

II

More and more Hassidim departed. In the
House of Study, on Saturdays, scarcely a quorum remained. The sextons, all but Avigdor,
had left. Finding her solitude unbearable, the
rabbi's wife went for a long visit to her brother,
the rabbi of Biala. Reb Abraham Moshe stayed
at Komarov. He spent one Sabbath each month

with his family in his native town. If a man
were not to be deserted when his body was sick,
he reasoned, then he certainly should not be left
alone during the sickness of his soul. If their
rabbi were committing sins, God forbid, then
one would be interdicted from associating with
him, but actually, his piety was now greater
than before. He prayed, studied, visited the ritual bathhouse. And he was so ardent in his
charity, that he sold his dearest possessions—
the silver candlesticks, the large Chanukah
candelabra, his gold watch, the Passover tray—
and gave the proceeds to the poor. Reb Abraham
Moshe told him reproachfully he was squan-
dering his inheritance, but the rabbi replied,
"Poor men *do* exist. That's one thing of which
we can be certain."

The summer went by and the month of Elul
came. On week days, Avigdor, the sexton, blew
the ram's horn at the House of Study. Komarov
used to be crowded to capacity during the month
of Elul; there were not enough beds at the inns,
and young people would sleep in storerooms,
barns, attics. But this year, it was quiet at Komarov. The shutters remained closed at the
inns. Grass grew wild in the rabbi's courtyard;
there was no one to trample it. Gossamer
threads floated through the air. The apples,
pears, and plums ripened on the trees in the
orchard, because the boys who used to pick them
were gone. The chirping of birds sounded louder
than ever. Moles dug up numerous mounds of

earth. Certain bushes sprouted berries of a poisonous sort. One day, the rabbi, on his way to the bathhouse, plucked one such berry. "If a thing like this can turn one into a corpse," he thought, "what is a corpse?" He sniffed it and threw it away. "If everything hinges on a berry, then all our affairs are berries." The rabbi entered the bathhouse. "Well, demons, where are you?" he said aloud, and his words were thrown back at him by the echo, "At least let there be devils." He sat on the bench, undressed, removed his fringed garment, and examined it. "Threads and knots and nothing else...."

The water was cold, but it made no difference to him. "Who is cold? And if one is cold, what of it?" The coldness cut his breath, and he clung to the railing. Then he plunged and stayed for a long while under the water. Something within him was laughing. "As long as you breathe, you must breathe." The rabbi dried himself and dressed. Returning to his study, he opened a Cabbala book, The Two Tablets of the Covenant. Here it was written that "the rigor of the law should be sweetened to deprive Satan of his nourishment." "Well, and what if it's a fairy tale?" The rabbi squinted one eye while the other kept staring. "The sun? Close your eyes and there is no sun. The birds? Stuff your ears and there are no birds. Pain? Swallow a wild berry, and the pain is gone. What is left, then? Nothing at all. The past no longer exists and the future has yet to come. The conclusion is that nothing exists beyond the moment. Well, if so, we really have nothing to worry about."

No more than thirty Hassidim gathered at Komarov for Rosh Hashona. Although the rabbi appeared at the service in his cloak and shawl, one could not tell if he prayed, for he was silent. After the service the Hassidim sat at the table, but their rabbi's seat was vacant. An old man chanted a little song and the others gave him a rattling accompaniment. Reb Abraham Moshe repeated a comment the rabbi had made on the Torah twenty years ago. Thank God, the rabbi was alive, though for all practical purposes, he was dead.

Avigdor brought to the rabbi's room a decanter of wine, apples with honey, the head of a carp, two challahs, a quarter of a chicken with stewed carrots, and a slice of pineapple for the blessing of the first fruit. But although it was already evening, the rabbi had touched nothing.

During the month of Elul he had fasted. His body felt as though it had been hollowed. Hunger still gnawed somewhere in his stomach, but it was a hunger unrelated to him. What had he, Bainish of Komarov, to do with food? Must one yield to the body's lusts? If one resists, what does it do—die? "Let it die, if that's what it wants. I am satisfied." A golden-green fly flew in through the open window from the other side of the curtain, and settled on the glazed eye of the carp. The rabbi murmured, "Well, what are you waiting for? Eat...."

As the rabbi sat half-awake, half-slumbering in his old chair, his arms on the arm rests, engrossed in thoughts he did not know he was thinking, divested of all external things, he suddenly caught sight of his youngest daughter, Rebecca. Through the closed door she had entered and stood there, erect, pale, her hair plaited in two tresses, wearing her best gold-embroidered dress, a prayer book in one hand, a handkerchief in the other. Forgetting that she had died, the rabbi looked at her, half-surprised. "See, she's a grown girl, how come she's not a bride?" An extraordinary nobility spread over her features; she looked as though she had just recovered from an illness; the pearls of her necklace shone with an unearthly light, with the aura of the Days of Awe. With an expression of modesty and love she gazed at the rabbi.

"Happy holiday, Father."

"Happy holiday, happy new year," the rabbi said.

"Father, say grace."

"What? Of course, of course."

"Father, join the guests at table," she said, half-commanding, half-imploring.

An icy shudder ran through the rabbi's spine. "But she's dead!" At once his eyes were drenched with tears, and he jumped to his feet as though to rush toward her. Through the mist of tears Rebecca's form became distorted, grew longer and partly blurred, but she still loomed before him. The rabbi noticed the silver clasp of her prayer book and the lace of her handkerchief.

Her left pigtail was tied with a white ribbon. But her face, as though veiled, dissolved into a blotch. The rabbi's voice broke.

"My daughter, are you here?"

"Yes, Father."

"Why have you come?"

"For you."

"When?"

"After the holidays."

She seemed to withdraw. In the whirling mist her form lost its substance, but her dress continued to drag on the floor in folds and waves like a golden train, and a glow arose from it. Soon this too dissolved, and nothing remained but a sense of wonder, a supernatural tang, a touch of heavenly joy. The rabbi did not weep, but luminous drops fell on his white silken robe embroidered with flowers and leaves. There was a fragrance of myrtle, cloves and saffron. He had a cloying sensation in his mouth, as if he had eaten marzipans.

The rabbi remembered what Rebecca had told him. He put on his fur hat, stood up, and opened the door leading to the House of Study. It was time for the evening prayer, but the old men had not yet left the table.

"Happy holiday, my friends," the rabbi said in a cheerful voice.

"Happy holiday, Rabbi."

"Avigdor, I want to say grace."

"I'm ready, Rabbi."

Avigdor brought the wine, and the rabbi,

chanting a holiday tune, recited the prayer. He washed his hands with the appropriate blessing and said the prayer for bread. After taking some broth, the rabbi commented on the Torah, a thing he had not done in years. His voice was low, though audible. The rabbi took up the question of why the moon is obscured on Rosh Hashona. The answer is that on Rosh Hashona one prays for life, and life means free choice, and freedom is Mystery. If one knew the truth how could there be freedom? If hell and paradise were in the middle of the market place, everyone would be a saint. Of all the blessings bestowed on man, the greatest lies in the fact that God's face is forever hidden from him. Men are the children of the Highest, and the Almighty plays hide and seek with them. He hides his face, and the children seek him while they have faith that He exists. But what if, God forbid, one loses faith? The wicked live on denials; denials in themselves are also a faith, faith in evil-doing, and from it one can draw strength for the body. But if the pious man loses his faith, the truth is shown to him, and he is recalled. This is the symbolic meaning of the words, "When a man dies in a tent": when the pious man falls from his rank, and becomes, like the wicked, without permanent shelter, then a light shines from above, and all doubts cease. . . .

The rabbi's voice gradually grew weaker. The old men leaned toward him, intently listening. The House of Study was so still that one could hear the candles flicker. Reb Abraham Moshe paled. He realized the meaning hidden behind all this. The moment Rosh Hashona was over, he mailed some letters, having sat until day-break writing them. The rabbi's wife returned from Biala, and for Yom Kippur the Hassidim arrived in great number. The rabbi had returned to his former self. During the Sukkoth holidays he commented on the Torah in his arbor. On Hashanah Raba he prayed all through the night, until dawn, with his Hassidim. On Simchas Torah, he never wearied of dancing around the reading stand. His Hassidim said later that Komarov had not, even under the old rabbi, blessed be his memory, celebrated that holiday with such gusto. To each of his Hassidim the rabbi spoke personally, asking about his family, and carefully reading each petition. He helped the children decorate the arbor with lanterns, ribbons, bunches of grapes. With his own hands, he wove baskets of lulab leaves for the myrtles. He pinched the cheeks of boys who had come with their fathers, and gave them cookies. As a rule, the rabbi prayed late and alone, but on the day following Succoth, he prayed in the House of Study with the first quorum. After the service he asked for a glass of coffee. Reb Abraham Moshe and a circle of young men stood watching the rabbi drink coffee. Between swallows, he puffed his pipe. He said, "I want you to know that the material world has no substance."

After breakfast, the rabbi said grace. Then
he ordered his bed made ready and murmured
something about his old prayer shawl. The moment he lay down he became moribund. His face
grew as yellow as his fringed garment. His
eyelids closed. Covered with wrinkles, his forehead assumed a strange aspect. Life could lit-
erally be seen departing from him; his body
shrank and altered. The rabbi's wife wanted to
call the doctor, but the rabbi signalled her not
to do so. Opening his eyes, he looked toward the
door. Between the door jambs, beside the *me-
zuseh,* all of them were standing—his four sons
and two daughters, his father, blessed be his
memory, and his grandfather. Reverently, they
all looked in his direction, expectantly, with
arms outstretched. Each of them emitted a different light. They bent forward as though restrained by an invisible fence. "So that's the
way it is," the rabbi thought, "Well, now everything is clear." He heard his wife sob, and
wanted to comfort her, but no strength remained in his throat and lips. Suddenly, Reb
Abraham Moshe leaned over him, as though
realizing that the rabbi wished to speak, and
the rabbi murmured, "One should always be
joyous."

Those were his final words.

Translated by Norbert Guterman
and Elaine Gottlieb

FROM THE DIARY
OF ONE NOT
BORN

I

Where man does not walk, where cattle do not
tread, Friday the thirteenth of the thirteenth
month, between day and night, behind the
Black Mountains, in the wasted woodland, at
the castle of Asmodeus, by the light of a
charmed moon.

I, the author of these lines, was blessed by a
good fortune that comes to only one in ten thousand: I was not born. My father, a yeshivah
student, sinned as did Onan, and from his seed
I was created—half spirit, half demon, half air,
half shade, horned like a buck and winged like
a bat, with the mind of a scholar and the heart
of a highwayman. I am and I am not. I whistle
down chimneys and dance in the public bath;
I overturn the pot of Sabbath food in a poor
man's kitchen; I make a woman unclean when
her husband returns from a trip. I like to play
all kinds of pranks. Once, when a young rabbi
was preaching his first sermon in the synagogue
on the Great Sabbath before the Passover, I
turned myself into a fly and bit the learned man
on the tip of his nose. He flicked me off, but I

flew to the lobe of his ear. He stretched out his
hand to drive me away, but I danced off onto
his high forehead, and paraded around between
the deep rabbinical furrows. He preached and
I sang, and I had the pleasure of hearing this
newly hatched scholar, still wet behind the ears,
scramble the text and forget the profundities
which he had expected to pour from his sleeve.
Oh yes, his enemies had a gay Sabbath! And
oh, how his wife berated him that evening! In-
deed, the quarrel between man and wife went
so far that, I blush to tell you, she would not
let him into her bed Passover night, when every
Jewish husband should be a king and every
Jewish wife, a queen. And if it had been destined for her to conceive Messiah then, I nipped
that in the bud!

Since my life span is eternal, and since I don't
have to worry about making a living, bringing
up children, or accounting for my deeds, I do
just as I please. Evenings, I watch the women
at the ritual baths, or make my way into the
bedrooms of pious folk and listen to the forbidden talk between man and wife. I enjoy reading
other people's letters and counting up the
amounts in women's nest-eggs. So sharp are my
ears that I can hear thoughts behind the skull,
and although I have no mouth and am dumb as
a fish, I can, when the occasion arises, make a
cutting remark. I have no need of money, but
I like to commit petty thieveries. I steal pins
from women's dresses and loosen their bows and

knots. I hide important papers and wills—what malicious deeds do I not do! For instance——

A Jewish landowner, Reb Paltiel, a learned man of a distinguished family and a charitable nature, became impoverished. His cows stopped giving milk, his land became barren, his bees made no more honey. Things went from bad to worse. Reb Paltiel could see that his luck was turning, and he said to himself, "Well—I'll die a poor man." He had a few volumes of the Talmud and a Psalter, so he sat down to study and pray, thinking, "The Lord giveth and the Lord taketh away. As long as I have bread I will eat, and when that, too, is gone, the time will have come to take a sack and a stick and go begging."

The man had a wife, Grene Peshe, and she had a wealthy brother, Reb Getz, in Warsaw. So she began to nag her husband, "What's the sense of sitting here and waiting until the last loaf is eaten? Go to Warsaw and tell my brother what has happened." Her husband was a proud man, however, and he replied, "I don't want any favors from anyone. If it is God's will that I be provided for, he will give me from his full hand, and if it is my fate to be a pauper, this trip will be a needless self-abasement."

But, as women have been given nine measures of garrulousness and only half a measure of faith, she pleaded and insisted until he capitulated. He put on his shabby fur coat with the moth-eaten foxtails, took a covered wagon to Reivitz, from thence to Lublin, and then he was bounced and jounced for days between Lublin and Warsaw.

The trip was long and arduous, the covered wagon jogging along for nearly a week. Nights, Reb Paltiel slept at wayside inns. It was right after the Feast of Tabernacles, when the skies are heavy with rain. The wagon wheels sank deep into the mire; their spokes were covered with mud. To make a long story short: the Warsaw Croesus, Reb Getz, grimaced, complained, bit his beard and muttered that new-found relatives, both on his side and on his wife's, were crawling out of the cracks in the walls. And finally he took out a five hundred gulden note, gave it to his needy brother-in-law, and bade him farewell, half warmly, half coldly, smiling and sighing, and asking to be remembered to his sister. A sister is, after all, a sister, one's own flesh and blood.

Reb Paltiel took the bank note, put it into his breast pocket, and started home. Truly, the humiliation he had suffered was worth more than five times five hundred gulden. But what's a man to do? Obviously, there's a time for honors and a time for indignities. And anyway, the indignities were in the past and the five hundred gulden were in his pocket. And with such a sum one could buy cows and horses and goats, and repair the roof and pay taxes, and take care of heaven knows how many other necessaries! I was right there (I happened, at the time, to be a flea in Reb Paltiel's beard), and I whispered to him, "Well, what do you say? The fact is that Grene Peshe isn't so crazy!" He answered me, "Evidently it was decreed. Who knows? Maybe heaven wanted me to atone for some sin, and from now on my luck will be better."

On the last night of the return trip, a heavy snow fell, and then there was a severe frost. The wagon couldn't move over the icy road, and Reb Paltiel had to take a sleigh. He arrived home frozen, exhausted from the long journey, hoarse and worn. He went into the house immediately. His wife, Grene Peshe, was sitting by the hearth warming herself. When she saw him she let out a shriek, "Woe is me—what you look like! I've seen them bury healthier looking specimens!" When he heard these lamentations, Reb Paltiel stuck his hand into his breast pocket, drew out the banknote, laid it down and announced, "Take it, it's yours." And he gave her the gift of charity which had cost him so much. Grene Peshe's face went from joy to gloom and back to joy. "So, well, I had expected a thousand," she said. "But five hundred isn't to be sneezed at, either."

And as she was saying these words, I sprang out of Reb Paltiel's beard and sat myself on Grene Peshe's nose. I jumped with such force that the poor woman dropped the paper, and it fell into the fire. And before either of them could cry out, a green and blue flame shot up, and of the five hundred gulden only an ash remained.

Well, what purpose will be served by telling

you what he said and what she answered? You can imagine it yourself. I leaped back into Reb Paltiel's beard, and stayed there until—and I hate to have to tell you this—he was forced to take a sack and a stick and go begging. Try to hang a flea! Try to run away from bad luck! Try to figure out where the evil spirit is!...

When I returned to the Black Mountains and told Asmodeus what I had done, he pinched my ear and repeated the story to his wife, Lilith, and she laughed with such abandon that the desert rang with the echoes of her glee, and she, herself, the Queen of Satan's Court, tweaked my nose:

"You're really a first rate little devil!" she said to me. "Some day you'll do big things!"

II

Where the heavens are copper and the earth iron, on a field of toadstools, in a ruined out-house, on a dung heap, in a pot without a bottom, on a Sabbath night during the winter solstice, not to be thought of now, nor later, nor at night, Amen-Selah!

The false prophecies of my mistress, Lilith, have been fulfilled. I am no longer an imp, but a full-grown devil—and a male, at that. I can disguise myself as a human, play my malicious pranks, and make men's eyes deceive them.

True, I can be driven off by a holy spell, but these days who knows Cabala? The little rabbis can pour salt on my tail. Their amulets are nothing but waste paper to me; their charms make me laugh. More than once I've left a souvenir of devil-dung in one of their skullcaps, or tied knots in their beards.

Yes, I do frightful things. I'm a demon among demons, an evil one among evil ones. One moonlit night I turned myself into a sack of salt and lay down by the roadside. Soon a wagon came along. Seeing the full sack, the driver stopped his horse, jumped out and hoisted me onto the cart. Who wouldn't take something for nothing? I was heavy as lead, and the ignoramus could hardly lift me. As soon as I was in the wagon, he opened the mouth of the sack and took a lick—evidently he wanted to find out whether I was salt or sugar. In a second I had become a calf, and I'll give you three guesses where he was licking me. When he saw what he was doing, the poor wretch nearly went crazy. His hands and feet began to tremble. "What's going on here?" he cried. "Where the devil am I?" Suddenly I flapped my wings and flew away like an eagle. The drayman arrived home a sick man. And now he goes around with an amulet and a piece of charmed amber, but they'll do him as much good as cupping a corpse.

One winter I came to the village of Turbin, in the form of a solicitor collecting for the needy in the Holy Land. I went from house to house, opening the metal alms-boxes which hung on the doors and taking out the small change, mostly worn half-pennies. From one of the houses came the smell of an overheated oven. The owner was a maiden in her thirties, both of whose parents were dead. She supported herself by baking cookies for the yeshiva students. She was short and stout, with a large bosom and an even larger what-do-you-call-it. The house was warm, the air redolent of cinnamon and poppy seeds, and it occurred to me that there would be nothing to be lost by marrying this old maid for a while. I smoothed my red sidelocks, combed my beard with my fingers, blew my frostbitten nose, and had a chat with the girl. One word led to another—I told her I was a childless widower. "I'm not a big earner, but I have a few hundred gulden in a purse beneath my fringed garment."

"Is your wife dead long?" she asks, and I answer, "It'll be three years the Fast of Esther."

She asks, "What was the matter with her?" and I reply, "She died in childbirth," and groan.

She can see that I'm an honest fellow—why else would a man mourn three years after his wife? In short, it's a match. The women of the town take the orphan under their wings. They collect a dowry for her. They supply her with tablecloths, napkins, sheets, shirts, petticoats, drawers. And since she is a virgin, they erect the wedding canopy in the synagogue court. The wedding presents are given, everyone dances with the newlyweds, and the bride is carried off to her bedroom. "Good luck!" the best man says to me. "I hope next year there'll be a circumcision feast!"

The guests leave. The night is long and dark. The bedroom is warm as an oven and black as Egypt. My bride is already in bed, under a down quilt—she had plucked the down herself—waiting for her husband. I grope around in the darkness; for the sake of appearances I undress, cough softly, and whisper to myself. "Are you tired?" I ask.

"Not so tired," she answers.

"You know," I say, "the other one, peace to her soul, was always tired. Poor thing, she was weak."

"Don't talk about her now," my wife admonishes. "May she put in a word for us in heaven."

"I want to tell you something," I say, "but don't get upset. On her deathbed she asked me to give her my holy word that I wouldn't marry again."

"You didn't promise?"

"Did I have any choice? You know it's forbidden to grieve the dying."

"You should have asked the rabbi what to do," the cookie baker says to me. "Why didn't you tell me earlier?"

"What's the matter, are you afraid she'll come back to choke you?"

"God forbid!" she answers. "How am I to blame? I knew nothing about it."

I get into bed, my body icy. "Why are you so cold?" my wife asks.

"Do you really want to know?" I say. "Come closer and I'll whisper it into your ear."

"Nobody can hear you," she says, astonished.

"There's a saying that the walls have ears," I reply.

She cocks her ear, and I spit right into it. She shudders and sits up. The bed boards squeak. The straw mattress begins to sag and crack.

"What are you doing?" she shrieks. "Is that supposed to be clever?"

Instead of answering, I begin to titter.

She says, "What kind of game is this? It may be all right for a child, but not for a grown man."

"And how do you know I'm not a child?" I answer. "I'm a child with a beard. Billy goats have beards, too."

"Well then," she says, "if you want to babble, babble. Good night."

And she turns her face to the wall. For a while we both lie quietly. And then I give her a pinch where she's fattest. My wife shoots up into the air. The bed shakes. She lets out a scream. "Are you crazy, or what? What are you pinching me for? Heaven help me—what kind of hands have I fallen into?"

And she begins to weep hoarsely—as can only a friendless orphan who has waited over thirty years for her lucky day and then finds herself espoused to a monster. A robber's heart would have melted. I'm sure that God himself shed a tear that night. But a devil is a devil.

At daybreak, I creep out of the house and go over to the rabbi's. The rabbi, a saintly man, is already at his studies, and is shocked to see me. "God bless a Jew," he says, "why so early?"

"It's true that I'm a stranger here, and only a poor man, but the town didn't have to wish a whore on me!"

"A whore!"

"What else is a bride who isn't a virgin?" I ask.

The rabbi tells me to wait for him in the study house and goes to wake up his wife. She gets dressed (even forgetting to wash her hands) and rouses some of her cronies. A little knot of women, including the rabbi's wife, goes over to my bride's to investigate and to look at the bed sheets. Turbin is no Sodom. If there's a sin, the town has to know about it!

My wife weeps bitterly. She swears that I hadn't come near her all night. She insists that I'm crazy, that I pinched her and spat in her ear, but the women shake their heads. They bring the defendant to the rabbi. They parade her through the market place, the townsfolk peering from every window. The study house is crowded. My wife moans and wails. She vows that no man has ever touched her, including me.

"He's a madman," she says, and turns on me. But I insist that she's lying.

"As a matter of fact," I announce, "let a doctor examine her."

"Where will we find a doctor in Turbin?" they ask.

"All right," I say, "then take her to Lublin. There's still some decency in the world," I screech. "I'll see to it that all of Poland hears about this! I'll tell the Rabinical Council the whole story!"

"Be sensible. How are we to blame?" asks one of the elders.

"It's the responsibility of all of Israel," I answer piously. "Whoever heard of a town letting a girl stay unmarried until she's over thirty and having her bake cookies for the yeshiva students?"

My wife realizes that I'm trying to ruin her business, too, and she rushes up to me with clenched fists. She's ready to hit me, and she would have, if she hadn't been restrained.

"Now, people," I scream. "See how shameless she is?"

By now it's apparent to everyone that I'm the honorable one, not she. In short, the rabbi says, "We still have a God in heaven. Divorce her and get rid of her."

"I beg your pardon," I say, "but I had expenses. The wedding cost me a good hundred gulden."

And so the bargaining begins. From her cookie baking my wife has managed to save, penny by penny, some seventy-odd gulden. They urge me to settle for that, but I'm adamant.

"Let her sell the wedding presents," I say.

And the girl shrieks, "Take everything! Tear out my insides!" And she claws at her face and cries out, "Oh, mother, I wish I were lying in the grave with you!" She beats her fists on the table, overturning the ink bottle, and sobs, "If this could happen to me, there's no God."

The beadle dashes over and slaps her, and she falls to the floor, her dress pulled up, her kerchief off her head. They try to lift her up, but she kicks, flails her arms and laments, "You're not Jews, but beasts!"

Nevertheless, that evening I collect my hundred gulden. The scribe sits down to write out the divorce papers. Suddenly I announce that I have to go out for a moment—and I never return. They search for me half the night. They call me, halloo after me; they hunt high and low. My wife becomes a permanent grass widow. And so, to spite God, the town and her own bad luck, she throws herself into the well.

Asmodeus himself praised my little job.

"Not bad," he said. "You're on the way." And he sent me to Machlath, the daughter of Namah, the she-devil who teaches young demons the paths of corruption.

Translated by Nancy Gross

THE OLD MAN

I

At the beginning of the Great War, Chaim Sachar of Krochmalna Street in Warsaw was a rich man. Having put aside dowries of a thousand rubles each for his daughters, he was about to rent a new apartment, large enough to include a Torah-studying son-in-law. There would also have to be additional room for his ninety-year-old father, Reb Moshe Ber, a Turisk hassid, who had recently come to live with him in Warsaw.

But two years later, Chaim Sachar's apartment was almost empty. No one knew where his two sons, young giants, who had been sent to the front, had been buried. His wife and two daughters had died of typhus. He had accompanied their bodies to the cemetery, reciting the memorial prayer for the three of them, preempting the most desirable place at the prayer stand in the synagogue, and inviting the enmity of other mourners, who accused him of taking unfair advantage of his multiple bereavement.

After the German occupation of Warsaw, Chaim Sachar, a tall, broad man of sixty who traded in live geese, locked his store. He sold his furniture by the piece, in order to buy frozen potatoes and moldy dried peas, and prepared gritty blackish noodles for himself and his father, who had survived the grandchildren.

Although Chaim Sachar had not for many months been near a live fowl, his large caftan was still covered with goose down, his great broad-brimmed hat glistened with fat, and his heavy, snub-toed boots were stained with slaughterhouse blood. Two small eyes, starved and frightened, peered from beneath his disheveled eyebrows; the red rims about his eyes were reminiscent of the time when he could wash down a dish of fried liver and hard-boiled eggs with a pint of vodka every morning after prayer. Now, all day long, he wandered through the market place, inhaling butchershop odors and those from restaurants, sniffing like a dog, and occasionally napping on porters' carts. With the refuse he had collected in a basket, he fed his kitchen stove at night; then, rolling the sleeves over his hairy arms, he would grate turnips on a grater. His father, meanwhile, sat warming himself at the open kitchen door, even though it was midsummer. An open Mishna treatise lay across his knees, and he complained constantly of hunger.

As though it were all his son's fault, the old man would mutter angrily, "I can't stand it much longer ... this gnawing...."

Without looking up from his book, a treatise on impurity, he would indicate the pit of his stomach and resume his mumbling in which the word "impure" recurred like a refrain. Although his eyes were a murky blue, like the eyes of a blind man, he needed no glasses, still retained some of his teeth, yellow and crooked as rusty nails, and awoke each day on the side on which he had fallen asleep. He was disturbed only by his rupture, which nevertheless, did not keep him from plodding through the streets of Warsaw with the help of his pointed stick, his "horse," as he called it. At every synagogue he would tell stories about wars, about evil spirits, and of the old days of cheap and abundant living when people dried sheepskins in cellars and drank spirits directly from the barrel through a straw. In return, Reb Moshe Ber was treated to raw carrots, slices of radish, and turnips. Finishing them in no time, he would then, with a trembling hand, pluck each crumb from his thinning beard—still not white—and speak of Hungary, where more than seventy years before, he had lived in his father-in-law's house. "Right after prayer, we were served a large decanter of wine and a side of veal. And with the soup there were hard-boiled eggs and crunchy noodles."

Hollow-cheeked men in rags, with ropes about their loins, stood about him, bent forward, mouths watering, digesting each of his words, the whites of their eyes greedily showing, as if the old man actually sat there eating. Young yeshiva students, faces emaciated from fasts, eyes shifty and restless as those of madmen, nervously twisted their long earlocks around their fingers, grimacing, as though to suppress stomach-aches, repeating ecstatically, "That was the time. A man had his share of heaven and earth. But now we have nothing."

For many months Reb Moshe Ber shuffled about searching for a bit of food; then, one night in late summer, on returning home, he found Chaim Sachar, his first-born, lying in bed, sick, barefoot, and without his caftan. Chaim Sachar's face was as red as though he had been to a steam bath, and his beard was crumpled in a knot. A neighbor woman came in, touched his forehead, and chanted, "Woe is me, it's that sickness. He must go to the hospital."

Next morning the black ambulance reappeared in the courtyard. Chaim Sachar was taken to the hospital; his apartment was sprayed with carbolic acid; and his father was led to the disinfection center, where they gave him a long white robe and shoes with wooden soles. The guards, who knew him well, gave him double portions of bread under the table and treated him to cigarettes. The Sukkoth holiday had passed by the time the old man, his shaven chin concealed beneath a kerchief, was allowed to leave the disinfection center. His son had died long before, and Reb Moshe Ber said the memorial prayer, *kaddish,* for him. Now alone in the apartment, he had to feed his stove with paper and wood shavings from garbage cans. In the ashes he baked rotten potatoes, which he carried in his scarf, and in an iron pot, he brewed chicory. He kept house, made his own candles by kneading bits of wax and suet around wicks, laundered his shirt beneath the kitchen faucet, and hung it to dry on a piece of string. He set the mousetraps each night and drowned the mice each morning. When he went out he never forgot to fasten the heavy padlock on the door. No one had to pay rent in Warsaw at that time. Moreover, he wore his son's boots and trousers. His old acquaintances in the Houses of Study, envied him. "He lives like a king!" they said, "He has inherited his son's fortune!"

The winter was difficult. There was no coal, and since several tiles were missing from the stove, the apartment was filled with thick black smoke each time the old man made a fire. A crust of blue ice and snow covered the window panes by November, making the rooms constantly dark or dusky. Overnight, the water on his night table froze in the pot. No matter how many clothes he piled over him in bed, he never felt warm; his feet remained stiff, and as soon as he began to doze, the entire pile of clothes would fall off, and he would have to climb out naked to make his bed once more. There was no kerosene; even matches were at a premium. Although he recited chapter upon chapter of the Psalms, he could not fall asleep. The wind, freely roaming about the rooms, banged the doors; even the mice left. When he hung up his shirt to dry, it would grow brittle and break, like glass. He stopped washing himself; his face became coal black. All day long he would sit in the House of Study, near the red-hot iron stove. On the shelves, the old books lay like piles of rags; tramps stood around the tin-topped tables, nondescript fellows with long matted hair and rags over their swollen feet—men who, having lost all they had in the war, were half-naked or covered only with torn clothes, bags slung over their shoulders. All day long, while orphans recited *kaddish,* women stood in throngs around the Holy Ark, loudly praying for the sick, and filling his ears with their moans and lamentations. The room, dim and stuffy, smelled like a mortuary chamber from the numerous anniversary candles that they were burning. Every time Reb Moshe Ber, his head hanging down, fell asleep, he would burn himself on the stove. He had to be escorted home at night, for his shoes were hobnailed, and he was afraid he might slip on the ice. The other tenants in his house had given him up for dead. "Poor thing— he's gone to pieces."

One December day, Reb Moshe Ber actually did slip, receiving a hard blow on his right arm.

The young man escorting him, hoisted Reb Moshe Ber on his back, and carried him home. Placing the old man on his bed without undressing him, the young man ran away as though he had committed a burglary. For two days the old man groaned, called for help, wept, but no one appeared. Several times each day he said his Confession of Sins, praying for death to come quickly, pounding his chest with his left hand. It was quiet outside in the daytime, as though everyone had died; a hazy green twilight came through the windows. At night he heard scratching noises as though a cat were trying to climb the walls; a hollow roar seemed to come repeatedly from underground. In the darkness the old man fancied that his bed stood in the middle of the room and all the windows were open. After sunset on the second day he thought he saw the door open suddenly, admitting a horse with a black sheet on its back. It had a head as long as a donkey's and innumerable eyes. The old man knew at once that this was the Angel of Death. Terrified, he fell from his bed, making such a racket that two neighbors heard it. There was a commotion in the courtyard; a crowd gathered, and an ambulance was summoned. When he came to his senses, Reb Moshe Ber found himself in a dark box, bandaged and covered up. He was sure this was his hearse, and it worried him that he had no heirs to say *kaddish,* and that therefore the peace of his grave would be disturbed. Suddenly he recalled the verses he would have to say to Duma, the Prosecuting Angel, and his bruised, swollen face twisted into a corpselike smile:

> *What man is he that liveth and shall not see death?*
> *Shall he deliver his soul from the grave?*

II

After Passover, Reb Moshe Ber was discharged from the hospital. Completely recovered, he once more had a great appetite but nothing to eat. All his possessions had been stolen; in the apartment only the peeling walls remained. He remembered Jozefow, a little village near the border of Galicia, where for fifty years he had lived and enjoyed great authority in the Turisk hassidic circle, because he had personally known the old rabbi. He inquired about the possibilities of getting there, but those he questioned merely shrugged their shoulders, and each said something different. Some assured him Jozefow had been burned to the ground, wiped out. A wandering beggar, on the other hand, who had visited the region, said that Jozefow was more prosperous than ever, that its inhabitants ate the Sabbath white bread even on week days.

But Jozefow was on the Austrian side of the border, and whenever Reb Moshe Ber broached the subject of his trip, men smiled mockingly in their beards and waved their hands. "Don't be foolish, Reb Moshe Ber. Even a young man couldn't do it."

But Reb Moshe Ber was hungry. All the turnips, carrots, and watery soups he had eaten in public kitchens had left him with a hollow sensation in his abdomen. All night he would dream of Jozefow knishes stuffed with ground meat and onions, of tasty concoctions of tripe and calf's feet, chicken fat and lean beef. The moment he closed his eyes he would find himself at some wedding or circumcision feast. Large brown rolls were piled up on the long table, and Turisk hassidim in silken caftans with high velvet hats over their skull caps, danced, glasses of brandy in their hands, singing:

> What's a poor man
> Cooking for his dinner?
> Borscht and potatoes!
> Borscht and potatoes!
> Faster, faster, hop-hop-hop!

He was the chief organizer of all those parties; he quarreled with the caterers, scolded the musicians, supervised every detail, and having no time to eat anything, had to postpone it all for later. His mouth watering, he awoke each morning, bitter that not even in his dream had he tasted those wonderful dishes. His heart pounded; his body was covered with a cold perspiration. The light outside seemed brighter every day, and in the morning, rectangular patterns of sunlight would waver on the peeling wall, swirling, as though they mirrored the rushing waves of a river close by. Around the bare hook for a chandelier on the crumbling ceiling, flies hummed. The cool golden glow of dawn illumined the window panes, and the distorted image of a bird in flight was always reflected in them. Beggars and cripples sang their songs in the courtyard below, playing their fiddles and blowing little brass trumpets. In his shirt, Reb Moshe Ber would crawl down from the one remaining bed, to warm his feet and stomach and to gaze at the barefoot girls in short petticoats who were beating red comforters. In all directions feathers flew, like white blossoms, and there were familiar scents of rotten straw and tar. The old man, straightening his crooked fingers, pricking up his long hairy ears as though to hear distant noises, thought for the thousandth time that if he didn't get out of here this very summer, he never would.

"God will help me," he would tell himself. "If he wills it, I'll be eating in a holiday arbor at Jozefow."

He wasted a lot of time at first by listening to people who told him to get a passport and apply for a visa. After being photographed, he was given a yellow card, and then he had to stand with hordes of others for weeks outside the Austrian consulate on a crooked little street somewhere near the Vistula. They were constantly being cursed in German and punched with the butts of guns by bearded, pipe-smoking soldiers. Women with infants in their arms wept and fainted. It was rumored that visas were granted only to prostitutes and to men who paid in gold. Reb Moshe Ber, going there every day at sunrise, sat on the ground and nodded over his Beni Issachar treatise, nourishing himself with grated turnips and moldy red radishes. But since the crowd continued to increase, he decided one day to give it all up. Selling his cotton-padded caftan to a peddler, he bought a loaf of bread, and a bag in which he placed his prayer shawl and phylacteries, as well as a few books for good luck; and planning to cross the border illegally, he set out on foot.

It took him five weeks to get to Ivangorod. During the day, while it was warm, he walked barefoot across the fields, his boots slung over his shoulders, peasant fashion. He fed on unripened grain and slept in barns. German military police often stopped him, scrutinized his Russian passport for a long time, searched him to see that he was not carrying contraband, and then let him go. At various times, as he walked, his intestines popped out of place; he lay on the ground and pushed them back with his hands.

In a village near Ivangorod he found a group
of Turisk hassidim, most of them young. When
they heard where he was going and that he
intended to enter Galicia, they gaped at him,
blinking, then, after whispering among themselves, they warned him, "You're taking a
chance in times like these. They'll send you to
the gallows on the slightest pretext."

Afraid to converse with him, lest the author-
ities grow suspicious, they gave him a few
marks and got rid of him. A few days later, in
that village, people spoke in hushed voices of
an old Jew who had been arrested somewhere
on the road and shot by a firing squad. But not
only was Reb Moshe alive by then; he was already on the Austrian side of the border. For
a few marks, a peasant had taken him across,
hidden in a cart under a load of straw. The old
man started immediately for Rajowiec. He fell
ill with dysentery there and lay in the poorhouse for several days. Everyone thought he
was dying, but he recovered gradually.

Now there was no shortage of food. Housewives treated Reb Moshe Ber to brown buckwheat with milk, and on Saturdays he even ate
cold calf's foot jelly and drank a glass of brandy.
The moment his strength returned, he was off
again. The roads were familiar here. In this
region, the peasants still wore the white linen
coats and quadrangular caps with tassels that
they had worn fifty years ago; they had beards

and spoke Ukrainian. In Zamosc the old man was arrested and thrown into jail with two young peasants. The police confiscated his bag. He refused gentile food and accepted only bread and water. Every other day he was summoned by the commandant who, as though Reb Moshe Ber were deaf, screamed directly into his ear in a throaty language. Comprehending nothing, Reb Moshe Ber simply nodded his head and tried to throw himself at the commandant's feet. This went on until after Rosh Hashonah; only then did the Zamosc Jews learn than an old man from abroad was being held in jail. The rabbi and the head of the community obtained his release by paying the commandant a ransom.

Reb Moshe Ber was invited to stay in Zamosc until after Yom Kippur, but he would not consider it. He spent the night there, took some bread, and set out on foot for Bilgorai at daybreak. Trudging across harvested fields, digging turnips for food, he refreshed himself in the thick pinewoods with whitish berries, large, sour and watery, which grow in damp places and are called Valakhi in the local dialect. A cart gave him a lift for a mile or so. A few miles from Bilgorai, he was thrown to the ground by some shepherds who pulled off his boots and ran away with them.

Reb Moshe Ber continued barefoot, and for this reason did not reach Bilgorai until late at night. A few tramps, spending the night in the House of Study, refused to let him in, and he had to sit on the steps, his weary head on his knees. The autumnal night was clear and cold; against the dark yellow, dull glow of the starry sky, a flock of goats, silently absorbed, peeled bark from the wood that had been piled in the synagogue courtyard for winter. As though complaining of an unforgettable sorrow, an owl lamented in a womanish voice, falling silent and then beginning again, over and over. People with wooden lanterns in their hands came at daybreak to say the *Selichoth* prayers. Bringing the old man inside, they placed him near the stove and covered him with discarded prayer shawls from the chest. Later in the morning they brought him a heavy pair of hobnailed, coarse-leathered military boots. The boots pinched the old man's feet badly, but Reb Moshe Ber was determined to observe the Yom Kippur fast at Jozefow, and Yom Kippur was only one day off.

He left early. There were no more than about four miles to travel, but he wanted to arrive at dawn, in time for the *Selichoth* prayers. The moment he had left town, however, his stiff boots began to cause him such pain, that he couldn't take a step. He had to pull them off and go barefoot. Then there was a downpour with thunder and lightning. He sank knee deep in puddles, kept stumbling, and became smeared with clay and mud. His feet swelled and bled. He spent the night on a haystack under the

open sky, and it was so cold that he couldn't
sleep. In the neighboring villages, dogs kept
barking, and the rain went on forever. Reb
Moshe Ber was sure his end had come. He
prayed God to spare him until the *Nilah* prayer,
so that he might reach heaven purified of all
sin. Later, when on the eastern horizon, the
edges of clouds began to glow, while the fog
grew milky white, Reb Moshe Ber was infused
with new strength and once again set off for
Jozefow.

He reached the Turisk circle at the very moment when the hassidim had assembled in the
customary way, to take brandy and cake. A few
recognized the new arrival at once, and there
was great rejoicing for he had long been thought
dead. They brought him hot tea. He said his
prayers quickly, ate a slice of white bread with
honey, gefilte fish made of fresh carp, and kreplach, and took a few glasses of brandy. Then he
was led to the steam bath. Two respectable citizens accompanied him to the seventh shelf and
personally whipped him with two bundles of
new twigs, while the old man wept for joy.

Several times during Yom Kippur, he was at
the point of fainting, but he observed the fast
until it ended. Next morning the Turisk hassidim gave him new clothes and told him to
study the Torah. All of them had plenty of
money, since they traded with Bosnian and
Hungarian soldiers, and sent flour to what had
been Galicia in exchange for smuggled tobacco.

It was no hardship for them to support Reb
Moshe Ber. The Turisk hassidim knew who he
was—a hassid who had sat at the table of no
less a man than Reb Motele of Chernobel! He
had actually been a guest at the famous wonder-
rabbi's home!

A few weeks later, the Turisk hassidim, timber merchants, just to shame their sworn enemies, the Sandzer hassidim, collected wood and
built a house for Reb Moshe Ber and married
him to a spinster, a deaf and dumb village girl
of about forty.

Exactly nine months later she gave birth to
a son—now he had someone to say *kaddish* for
him. As though it were a wedding, musicians
played at the circumcision ceremony. Well-to-
do housewives baked cakes and looked after the
mother. The place where the banquet was held,
the assembly room of the Turisk circle, smelled
of cinnamon, safron, and the women's best Sabbath dresses. Reb Moshe Ber wore a new satin
caftan and a high velvet hat. He danced on the
table, and for the first time, mentioned his age:

"And Abraham was a hundred years old," he
recited, "when his son Isaac was born unto him.
And Sarah said: God hath made me laugh so
that all who hear will laugh with me."

He named the boy Isaac.

Translated by Norbert Guterman
and Elaine Gottlieb

FIRE

I want to tell you a story. It isn't from a book—
it happened to me personally. I've kept it secret
all these years, but I know now I'll never leave
this poorhouse alive. I'll be carried straight
from here to the morgue. So I want the truth
known. I'd have had the rabbi and the town
elders here, and got them to record it in the
community book, but why embarrass my
brother's children and grandchildren? Here is
my story.

I come from Janow near Zomosc. The place
is called Poorman's Kingdom, for obvious reasons. My father, God bless his memory, had
seven children, but lost five of them. They grew
up strong as oaks and then down they fell. Three
boys and two girls! No one knew what was
wrong. The fever got them one after the other.
When Chaim Jonah, the youngest, died, my
mother—may she intercede for me in heaven—
went out like a candle. She wasn't ill, she just
stopped eating and stayed in bed. Neighbors
dropped in and asked, "Beile Rivke, what's
wrong?" and she answered, "Nothing. I'm just

going to die." The doctor came and she was bled; they applied cups and leeches, exorcised the evil eye, washed her with urine, but nothing worked. She shriveled up until she was nothing but a bag of bones. When she had said her Confession of Sins she called me to her side. "Your brother Lippe will make his way in the world," she said, "but you, Leibus, I pity."

Father never liked me. I don't know why. Lippe was taller than me, he took after Mother's family. He was smart in school though he didn't study. I studied, but it didn't help. What I heard went in one ear and out the other. Even so I can find my way around in the Bible. I was soon taken out of *cheder*.

My brother Lippe was, as the saying goes, the apple of Father's eye. When my brother did something wrong, Father looked the other way, but God forbid that I should make a mistake. He had a weighty hand; every time he smacked me I saw my dead grandmother. As far back as I can remember it was like that. The slightest thing and off came his belt. He beat me black and blue. It was always, "Don't go here, don't go there." In the synagogue, for example, all the other boys fooled around during the services, but if I left out a single "Amen," I got my "reward." At home I did all the work. We had a handmill, and all day long I ground buckwheat; I was also water-carrier and wood-chopper; I made the fire and cleaned the outhouse.

Mother protected me while she was alive, but after she was gone, I was a stepchild. Don't think it didn't eat into me, but what could I do? My brother Lippe shoved me around too.—"Leibus, do this. Leibus, do that."—Lippe had his friends; he liked to drink; he hung around the tavern.

There was a pretty girl in our town, Havele. Her father owned a drygoods store. He was well fixed, and he had his ideas about a son-in-law. My brother had other ideas. He set his trap carefully. He paid the matchmakers not to bring her proposals. He spread a rumor that someone in her family had hanged himself. His friends helped out, and in return they got their share of brandy and poppy seed cake. Money was no problem for him. He just opened Father's drawer and took what he pleased. In the end Havele's father was beaten down, and gave consent to the marriage to Lippe.

The whole town celebrated the engagement. The bridegroom does not usually bring a dowry, but Lippe persuaded Father to give him two hundred gulden. He also got a wardrobe fit for a landlord. At the wedding there were two bands, one from Janow and one from Bilgorai. That is how he started on his way up. But it was different for the younger brother; he didn't even get a new pair of pants. Father had promised me clothes, but he put off ordering from day to day, and by the time he had bought the

material it was too late to have it made up. I
went to the wedding in rags. The girls laughed
at me. Such was my luck.

I thought I would go the way of my other
brothers and sisters. But I was not fated to die.
Lippe got married; as the saying goes, he
started off on the right foot. He became a suc-
cessful dealer in grain. Near Janow there was
a watermill belonging to Reb Israel David, son
of Malka, a fine man. Israel David took a liking
to my brother and sold him the mill for a song.
I don't know why he sold it; some said that he
wanted to go to the Holy Land, others that he
had relatives in Hungary. Whatever the reason,
shortly after selling the mill, he died.

Havele had one child after another, each pret-
tier than the last; they were such marvels, people came just to look at them. The dowry Father
had given Lippe undermined his own business;
he was left without a cent. The business collapsed, as well as his strength, but if you think
that my brother Lippe gave him a helping hand,
you're very much mistaken. Lippe neither saw
nor heard anything, and Father took his bit-
terness out on me. What he had against me I
don't know; sometimes a man conceives such a
hatred for his child. No matter what I said, it
was wrong, and no matter how much I did, it
was not enough.

Then Father fell ill, and everyone could see
he would not last long. My brother Lippe was

busy making money. I took care of Father. It
was I who carried the bedpan; it was I who
washed, bathed, combed him. He couldn't digest
anything; he kept spitting up whatever he ate.
The disease spread to his legs too, so he couldn't
walk. I had to bring him everything, and whenever he saw me he looked at me as though I
were dirt. Sometimes he wore me out so that I
wanted to run from him to the end of the world,
but how can you leave your own father? And so
I suffered in silence. The final weeks were just
hell: Father swearing and groaning. I have
never heard more horrible curses. My brother
Lippe would drop in twice a week and ask with
a smile, "Well, how are you, Father? No better?"
and the moment Father saw him, his eyes
brightened. I have forgiven him, and may God
forgive him too: does a man know what he is
doing?

It took him two weeks to die and I can't begin
to describe his agony. Every time he opened his
eyes he stared at me in rage. After the funeral,
his will was found under a pillow; I was dis-
possessed. Everything was left to Lippe—the
house, the handmill, the cupboard, the chest of
drawers, even the dishes. The town was shocked;
such a will, people said, was illegal. There was
even a precedent to this effect in the Talmud.
It was suggested that Lippe give me the house,
but he merely laughed. Instead he sold it immediately, and moved the handmill and the furniture to his own place. I was left the pillow.

This is the truth pure and simple. May I be no less pure when I come before God!

I began to work for a carpenter and I could scarcely earn a living. I slept in a shed; Lippe forgot that he had a brother. But who do you suppose said *kaddish* for Father? There was always some reason why it couldn't be Lippe: I lived in town, there weren't enough men at the mill for the service, it was too far away for him to get to *shul* on Saturday. At first they gossiped about his treatment of me, but then people began to say he must have his reasons. When a man is down, everyone likes to walk on him.

I was now no longer young and still unmarried. I had grown a beard but no one thought of a match for me. If a matchmaker did come, what he offered was the dregs of the dregs. But why should I deny it, I did fall in love. The girl was the cobbler's daughter and I used to watch her emptying slops. But she became engaged to a cooper. Who wants an orphan? I was no fool; it hurt. Sometimes I couldn't sleep at night. I would toss about in my bed as if I had a fever. Why? What had I done to my father? I decided that I would stop saying *kaddish,* but a year had almost gone by. Besides how can you take revenge on the dead?

And now let me tell you what happened.

One Friday night I lay in my shed on a pile of shavings. I had worked hard; in those days

one began at dawn, and the price of the candle
was deducted from one's wages. I hadn't even
had time to go to the bathhouse. On Fridays we
got no lunch, so we should have a keener appetite for the Sabbath dinner, but at dinner the
carpenter's wife always dished out less to me
than to the others. Everyone else got a nice
piece of fish, I got the tail. I would choke on the
first mouthful of bone. The soup was watery,
and my portion of meat was the chicken legs,
along with some strings of muscle. It was not
only that you couldn't chew it, but if you swallowed it, according to the Talmud, it weakened
your memory. I didn't even get enough *challah,*
and as for any of the sweets, I never got a taste.
So I had gone to sleep hungry.

It was winter, and bitter cold in my shed.
There was an awful racket—the mice. I lay on
my pile of shavings, with rags for covers, burning with rage. What I wanted was to get my
hands on my brother Lippe. Havele also came
into my mind; you might expect a sister-in-law
to be kinder than a brother, but she had time
only for herself and her little dolls. The way she
dressed you would have thought she was a great
lady; the few times she came to *shul* to attend
a wedding, she wore a plumed hat. Wherever
I went I would hear told how Lippe had bought
this, Havele had bought that; their main business, it seemed, was adorning themselves. She
treated herself to a skunk coat, and then to a
fox fur; she paraded herself in flounces while

I lay like a dog, my belly growling with hunger. I cursed them both. I prayed that God would send them plagues, and everything else I could think of. Gradually I fell asleep.

But then I awoke; it was the middle of the night and I felt that I must take revenge. It was as if some devil had seized me by the hair and shouted, "Leibus, it is time for revenge!" I got up; in the darkness I found a bag which I filled with shavings. Such things are forbidden on the Sabbath, but I had forgotten my religion: surely there was a *dybbuk* in me. I dressed quietly, took the bag with the shavings, two flints and a wick, and sneaked out. I would set fire to my brother's house, the mill, the granary, everything.

It was pitch dark out and I had a long way to go. I kept away from the town. I cut across swampy pastures, over fields and meadows. I knew that I would lose everything—this world and the next. I even thought of my mother lying in her grave: what would she say? But when you're mad you can't stop. You bite off your tongue to spite your face, as the saying goes. I wasn't even worried about running into someone I knew. I just wasn't myself.

I walked and walked, and the wind blew; the cold cut into me. I sank into snow over my knees, and climbed out of one ditch only to fall into another. As I passed by the hamlet known as "The Pines," dogs attacked me. You know how it is: when one dog barks, all the rest join

in. I was pursued by a pack, and I thought I
would be torn to pieces. It was a miracle that
the peasants didn't wake and take me for a
horse thief; they would have done away with
me on the spot. I was on the verge of giving up
the whole thing; I wanted to drop the bag and
hurry back to bed. Or I thought of simply wandering away, but my *dybbuk* kept inciting me:
"Now or never!" I trudged on and on. Wood
shavings aren't heavy, but if you carry a bagful
long enough you feel it. I began to sweat, but
I kept on going at the risk of my life.

And now listen to this coincidence.

As I walked I suddenly saw a red glow in the
sky. Could it be dawn? No, that didn't seem
possible. It was early winter; the nights were
long. I was very close to the mill and I walked
faster. I almost ran. Well, to make a long story
short, I arrived at the mill to find it on fire. Can
you imagine that? I had come to set a building
on fire and it was already burning. I stood as
though paralyzed, with my head spinning; it
seemed to me that I was losing my mind. Maybe
I was: for the very next moment I threw down
my bag of shavings and began to scream for
help. I was about to run to the mill when I
remembered Lippe and his family, and so I
rushed to the house; it was a blazing inferno.
It seemed they had all been overcome by smoke.
Beams were burning; it was as bright as on
Simchas Torah. Inside it felt like an oven, but

I ran to the bedroom, smashed open a window, seized my brother, and threw him into the snow. I did the same with his wife and children. I almost choked to death but I rescued them all. No sooner had I finished, than the roof collapsed. My screams had awakened the peasants and now they came running. They revived my brother and his family. The chimney and a pile of ashes were all that was left of the house but the peasants managed to put out the fire in the mill. I caught sight of the bag of shavings and threw it into the fire. My brother and his family found shelter with some neighbors. By this time it was daylight.

My brother's first question was, "How did it happen? How come you're here?" My sister-in-law rushed at me to scratch my eyes out. "He did it! He set the fire!" The peasants also questioned me, "What devil brought you here?" I didn't know what to say. They began to club me. Just before I was battered to a pulp, my brother held up his hand, "No more, neighbors. There is a God and He'll punish him," and with that he spat in my face.

Somehow or other I managed to get home; I didn't walk, I dragged myself. Like a crippled animal I pulled myself along on all fours. A few times I paused to cool my wounds in the snow. But when I got home my real troubles began. Everyone asked, "Where were you? How come you knew your brother's house was on fire?" Then they learned that I was suspected. The man I worked for came to my shed and raised the roof when he found that one of his bags was missing. All Janow said that I had set my brother's house on fire, and on the Sabbath no less.

Things couldn't have been worse. I was in danger of being jailed, or pilloried in the synagogue yard. I didn't wait, I made myself scarce. A carter took pity on me and drove me to Zamosc that Saturday night. He carried no passengers, only freight, and he squeezed me in among the barrels. When the story of the fire reached Zamosc, I left for Lublin. There I became a carpenter and married. My wife bore me no children; I worked hard but I had no luck. My brother Lippe became a millionaire—he owned half of Janow—but I never had a line from him. His children married rabbis and wealthy businessmen. He is no longer alive—he died weighted down with riches and honors.

Until now I have told this story to no one. Who would have believed it? I even kept it a secret that I was from Janow. I always said that I was from Shebreshin. But now that I'm on my deathbed, why should I lie? What I've told is the truth, the whole whole truth. There's only one thing I don't understand and won't understand it until I'm in my grace: why did a fire have to break out in my brother's house on just that night? Some time ago it occurred to me that it was my anger that started that fire. What do you think?

"Anger won't make a house burn."

"I know.... Still there's that expression, 'burning anger!'"

"Oh, that's just a way of talking."

Well, when I saw that fire I forgot everything and rushed to save them. Without me they would have all been ashes. Now that I'm about to die, I want the truth known.

Translated by Norbert Guterman

THE UNSEEN

I

Nathan and Temerl

They say that I, the Evil Spirit, after descending to earth in order to induce people to sin, will then ascend to heaven to accuse them. As a matter of fact, I am also the one to give the sinner the first push, but I do this so cleverly that the sin appears to be an act of virtue; thus, other infidels, unable to learn from the example, continue to sink into the abyss.

But let me tell you a story. There once lived a man in the town of Frampol who was known for his wealth and lavish ways. Named Nathan Jozefover, for he was born in Little Jozefov, he had married a Frampol girl and settled there. Reb Nathan, at the time of this story, was sixty, perhaps a bit more. Short and broad-boned, he had, like most rich people, a large paunch. Cheeks red as wine showed between the clumps of short black beard. Over small twinkling eyes his eyebrows were thick and shaggy. All his life, he had eaten, drunk, and made merry. For breakfast, his wife served him cold chicken and raisin bread, which, like a great landowner, he washed down with a glass of mead. He had a preference for dainties such as roast squab, necks stuffed with chopped milt, pancakes with liver, egg noodles with broth, etc. The towns-people whispered that his jwife, Roise Temerl, prepared a noodle-pudding for him every day, and if he so desired made a Sabbath dinner in the middle of the week. Actually, she too liked to indulge.

Having plenty of money and no children, hus-band and wife apparently believed that good cheer was in order. Both of them, therefore, be-came fat and lazy. After their lunch, they would close the bedroom shutters and snore in their featherbeds as though it were midnight. During the winter nights, long as Jewish exile, they would get out of bed to treat themselves to giz-zard, chicken livers, and jam, washed down with beet soup or apple juice. Then, back to their canopied beds they went to resume their dreams of the next day's porridge.

Reb Nathan gave little time to his grain busi-ness, which ran itself. A large granary with two oaken doors stood behind the house he had in-herited from his father-in-law. In the yard there were also a number of barns, sheds, and other buildings. Many of the old peasants in the sur-rounding villages would sell their grain and flax to Nathan alone, for, even though others might offer them more, they trusted Nathan's honesty. He never sent anyone away empty-handed, and sometimes even advanced money for the following year's crop. The simple peas-ants, in gratitude, brought him wood from the forest, while their wives picked mushrooms and berries for him. An elderly servant, widowed in her youth, looked after the house and even assisted in the business. For the entire week, with the exception of market day, Nathan did not have to lift a finger.

He enjoyed wearing fine clothes and telling yarns. In the summer, he would nap on a bed among the trees of his orchard, or read either the Bible in Yiddish, or simply a story book. He liked, on the Sabbath, to listen to the preaching of a *magid*, and occasionally to invite a poor man to his house. He had many amusements: for example, he loved to have his wife, Roise Temerl, tickle his feet, and she did this whenever he wished. It was rumored that he and his wife would bathe together in his own bathhouse, which stood in his yard. In a silk dressing gown embroidered with flowers and leaves, and wearing pompommed slippers, he would step out on his porch in the afternoon, smoking a pipe with an amber bowl. Those who passed by greeted him, and he responded in a friendly fashion. Sometimes he would stop a passing girl, ask her this and that, and then send her off with a joke. After the reading of the *Perek* on Saturday, he would sit with the women on the bench, eating nuts or pumpkin seeds, listening to gossip, and telling of his own encounters with landowners, priests, and rabbis. He had traveled widely in his youth, visiting Cracow, Brody, and Danzig.

Roise Temerl was almost the image of her husband. As the saying goes: when a husband and wife sleep on one pillow finally they have the same head. Small and plump, she had cheeks still full and red despite her age, and a tiny talkative mouth. The smattering of Hebrew, with which she just found her way through the prayer books, gave her the right to a leading role in the women's section of the Prayer House. She often led a bride to the synagogue, was sponsor at a circumcision, and occasionally collected money for a poor girl's trousseau. Although a wealthy woman, she could apply cups to the sick, and would adroitly cut out the pip of a chicken. Her skills included embroidery and knitting. She possessed numerous jewels, dresses, coats, and furs, all of which she kept in oaken chests as protection against moths and thieves.

Because of her gracious manner, she was welcomed at the butcher's, at the ritual bath, and wherever else she went. Her only regret was that she had no children. To make up for this, she gave charitable contributions and engaged a pious scholar to pray in her memory after her death. She took pleasure in a nest-egg she had managed to save over the years, kept it hidden somewhere in a bag, and now and then enjoyed counting the gold pieces. However, since Nathan gave her everything she needed, she had no idea of how to spend the money. Although he knew of her hoard, he pretended ignorance, realizing that "stolen water is sweet to drink," and did not begrudge her this harmless diversion.

II

Shifra Zirel the Servant

One day their old servant became ill and soon died. Nathan and his wife were deeply grieved, not only because they had grown so accustomed to her that she was almost a blood relative, but she had also been honest, industrious, and loyal, and it would not be easy to replace her. Nathan and Roise Temerl wept over her grave, and Nathan said the first *kaddish*. He promised that after the thirty day mourning period, he would drive to Janow to order the tombstone she deserved. Nathan actually did not come out a loser through her death. Having rarely spent any of her earnings, and being without a family, she had left everything to her employers.

Immediately after the funeral, Roise Temerl began to look for a new servant, but could not find any that compared to the first. The Frampol girls were not only lazy, but they could not bake and fry to Roise Temerl's satisfaction. Various widows, divorced women, and deserted wives were offered her, but none had the qualifications that Roise Temerl desired. Of every candidate presented at her house, she would make inquiries on how to prepare fish, marinate borscht, bake pastry, struddle, egg cookies, etc.; what to do when milk and borscht sour, when a chicken is too tough, a broth too fat, a Sabbath pudding overdone, a porridge too thick or too thin, and other tricky questions. The bewildered girl would lose her tongue and leave in embarrassment. Several weeks went by like this, and the pampered Roise Temerl, who had to do all the chores, could clearly see that it was easier to eat a meal than prepare one.

Well, I, the Seducer, could not stand by and watch Nathan and his wife starve; I sent them a servant, a wonder of wonders.

A native of Zamosc, she had even worked for wealthy families in Lublin. Although at first she had refused—even if she were paid her weight in gold—to go to an insignificant spot like Frampol, various people had intervened, Roise Temerl had agreed to pay a few gulden more than she had paid previously, and the girl, Shifra Zirel, decided to take the job.

In the carriage that had to be sent to Zamosc for her and her extensive luggage, she arrived with suitcases, baskets, and knapsacks, like a rich bride. Well along in her twenties, she seemed no more than eighteen or nineteen. Her hair was plaited in two braids coiled at the sides of her head; she wore a checkered shawl with tassels, a cretonne dress, and narrow heeled shoes. Her chin had a wolf-like sharpness, her lips were thin, her eyes shrewd and impudent.

She wore rings in her ears and around her throat a coral necklace. Immediately, she found fault with the Frampol mud, the clay taste of the well water, and the lumpy home-made bread. Served over-cooked soup by Roise Temerl on the first day, she took a drop of it with her spoon, made a face, and complained, "It's sour and rancid!"

She demanded a Jewish or Gentile girl as an assistant, and Roise Temerl, after a strenuous search, found a Gentile one, the sturdy daughter of the bath attendant. Shifra Zirel began to give orders. She told the girl to scrub the floors, clean the stove, sweep the cobwebs in corners, and advised Roise Temerl to get rid of the superfluous pieces of furniture, various rickety chairs, stools, tables, and chests. The windows were cleaned, the dusty curtains removed, and the rooms became lighter and more spacious. Roise Temerl and Nathan were amazed by her first meal. Even the emperor could ask for no better cook. An appetizer of calves' liver and lungs, partly fried and partly boiled, was served before the broth, and its aroma titillated their nostrils. The soup was seasoned with herbs unobtainable at Frampol, such as paprika and capers, which the new servant had apparently brought from Zamosc. Dessert was a mixture of applesauce, raisins, and apricots, flavored with cinnamon, saffron, and cloves, whose fragrance filled the house. Then, as in the wealthy homes of Lublin, she served black coffee with chicory. After lunch, Nathan and his wife wanted to nap as usual, but Shifra Zirel warned them that it was unhealthful to sleep immediately after eating, because the vapors mount from the stomach to the brain. She advised her employers to walk back and forth in the garden a few times. Nathan was brimful of good food, and the coffee had gone to his head. He reeled and kept repeating, "Well, my dear wife, isn't she a treasure of a servant?"

"I hope no one will take her away," Roise Temerl said. Knowing how envious people were, she feared the Evil Eye, or those who might offer the girl better terms.

There is no sense going into detail about the excellent dishes Shifra Zirel prepared, the babkas and macaroons she baked, the appetizers she introduced. The neighbors found Nathan's rooms and his yard unrecognizable. Shifra Zirel had whitewashed the walls, cleaned the sheds and closets, and hired a laborer to weed the garden and repair the fence and railing of the porch. Like the mistress of the house rather than its servant, she supervised everything. When Shifra Zirel, in a woolen dress and pointed shoes, went for a stroll on Saturdays, after the pre-cooked *cholent* dinner, she was stared at not only by common laborers and poor girls, but by young men and women of good families as well. Daintily holding up her skirt, she walked, her head high. Her assistant, the bathhouse attendant's daughter, followed, carrying a bag of fruit and cookies, for Jews could not carry parcels on the Sabbath. From the benches in front of their houses women observed her and shook their heads. "She's as proud as a landowner's wife!" they would comment, predicting that her stay in Frampol would be brief.

III

Temptation

One Tuesday, when Roise Temerl was in Janow visiting her sister, who was ill, Nathan ordered the Gentile girl to prepare a steam bath for him. His limbs and bones had been aching since morning, and he knew that the only remedy for this was to perspire abundantly. After putting a great deal of wood in the stove around the bricks, the girl lighted the fire, filled the vat with water, and returned to the kitchen.

When the fire had burnt itself out, Nathan undressed and then poured a bucket of water on the red hot bricks. The bathhouse filled with steam. Nathan, climbing the stairs to the high shelf where the steam was hot and dense, whipped himself with a twig broom that he had prepared previously. Usually Roise Temerl helped him with this. When he perspired she poured the buckets of water, and when she perspired he poured. After they had flogged each other with twig brooms, Roise Temerl would bathe him in a wooden tub and comb him. But this time Roise Temerl had had to go to Janow to her sick sister, and Nathan did not think it wise to wait for her return, since his sister-in-law was very old and might die and then Roise Temerl would have to stay there seven days. Never before had he taken his bath alone. The steam, as usual, soon settled. Nathan wanted to go down and pour more water on the bricks, but his legs felt heavy and he was lazy. With his belly protruding upward, he lay on his back, flogging himself with the broom, rubbing his knees and ankles, and staring at the bent beam on the smoke-blackened ceiling. Through the crack, a patch of clear sky stared in. This was the month of Elul, and Nathan was assailed by melancholy. He remembered his sister-in-law as a young woman full of life, and now she was on her deathbed. He too would not eat marchpanes nor sleep on eiderdown forever, it occurred to him, for some day he would be placed in a dark grave, his eyes covered with shards, and worms would consume the body that Roise Temerl had pampered for the nearly fifty years that she had been his wife.

Probing his soul, Nathan lay there, belly upward, when he suddenly heard the chain clank, the door creak. Looking about, he saw to his amazement, that Shifra Zirel had entered.

Barefoot, with a white kerchief around her head, she was dressed only in a slip. In a choking voice, he cried out, "No!" and hastened to cover himself. Upset, and shaking his head, he beckoned her to leave, but Shifra Zirel said, "Don't be afraid, master, I won't bite you."

She poured a bucket of water over the hot bricks. A hissing noise filled the room, and white clouds of steam quickly rose, scalding Nathan's limbs. Then Shifra Zirel climbed the steps to Nathan, grabbed the twig broom, and began to flog him. He was so stunned, he became speechless. Choking, he almost rolled off the slippery shelf. Shifra Zirel, meanwhile, continued diligently to whip him and to rub him with a cake of soap she had brought. Finally, having regained his composure, he said, hoarsely, "What's the matter with you? Shame on you!"

"What's there to be ashamed about?" the servant asked airily, "I won't harm the master..."

For a long time she occupied herself combing and massaging him, rubbing him with soap, and drenching him with water, and Nathan was compelled to acknowledge that this devilish woman was more accomplished than Roise Temerl. Her hands, too, were smoother; they tickled his body and aroused his desire. He soon forgot that this was the month of Elul, before the Days of Awe, and told the servant to lock the wooden latch of the door. Then, in a wavering voice, he made a proposition.

"Never, uncle!" she said resolutely, pouring a bucket of water on him.

"Why not?" he asked, his neck, belly, head, all his limbs dripping.

"Because I belong to my husband."

"What husband?"

"The one I'll have some day, God willing."

"Come on, Shifra Zirel," he said, "I'll give you something—a coral necklace, or a brooch."

"You're wasting your breath," she said.

"A kiss at least!" he begged.

"A kiss will cost twenty-five coins," Shifra Zirel said.

"Groszy or threepence pieces?" Nathan asked, efficiently, and Shifra Zirel answered, "Gulden."

Nathan reflected. Twenty-five gulden was no trifle. But I, the Old Nick, reminded him that one does not live forever, and that there was no harm in leaving a few gulden less behind. Therefore, he agreed.

Bending over him, placing her arms about his neck, Shifra Zirel kissed him on the mouth. Half kiss and half bite, it cut his breath. Lust arose in him. He could not climb down, for his arms and legs were trembling, and Shifra Zirel had to help him down and even put on his dressing gown. "So that's the kind you are..." he murmured.

"Don't insult me, Reb Nathan," she admonished, "I'm pure."

"Pure as a pig's knuckle," Nathan thought.

He opened the door for her. After a moment, glancing anxiously about to make sure he was not seen, he left also. "Imagine such a thing happening!" he murmured. "What impudence! A real whore!" He resolved never again to have anything to do with her.

IV

Troubled Nights

Nathan lay at night on his eiderdown mattress, wrapped in a silken blanket, his head propped up by three pillows, but he was robbed of sleep by my wife Lilith and her companions. He had droused off, but was awake; he began to dream something, but the vision frightened him, and he rose with a start. Someone invisible whispered something into his ear. He fancied, for a moment, that he was thirsty. Then his head felt feverish. Leaving his bed, he slipped into his slippers and dressing gown, and went to the kitchen to scoop up a mug of water. Leaning over the barrel, he slipped and almost fell in. Suddenly he realized that he craved Shifra Zirel with the craving of a young man. "What's the matter with me?" he murmured, "This can only be a trick of the devil." He started to walk to his own room, but found himself going to the little room where the servant slept. Halting at the doorway, he listened. A rustling came from behind the stove, and in the dry wood something creaked. The pale glow of a lantern flashed outside; there was a sigh. Nathan recalled that this was Elul, that God-fearing Jews rise at dawn for the *Selichot* prayers. Just as he was about to turn back, the servant opened the door and asked in an alert tone, "Who's there?"

"I am," Nathan whispered.

"What does the master wish?"

"Don't you know?"

She groaned and was silent, as though wondering what to do. Then she said, "Go back to bed, master. It's no use talking."

"But I can't sleep," Nathan complained in a tone he sometimes used with Roise Temerl, "Don't send me away!"

"Leave, master," Shifra Zirel said in an angry voice, "or I'll scream!"

"Hush. I won't force you, God forbid. I'm fond of you. I love you."

"If the master loves me then let him marry me."

"How can I? I have a wife!" Nathan said, surprised.

"Well, what of it? What do you think divorce is for?" she said and sat up.

"She's not a woman," Nathan thought, "but a demon." Frightened by her and her talk he remained in the doorway, heavy, bewildered, leaning against the jamb. The Good Spirit, who is at the height of his power during the month of Elul, reminded him of *The Measure of Right-*

eousness—which he had read in Yiddish—stories of pious men, tempted by landowners' wives, she-demons, whores, but who refused to succumb to the temptation. "I'll send her away at once, tomorrow, even if I must pay her wages for a year," Nathan decided. But he said, "What's wrong with you? I've lived with my wife for almost fifty years! Why should I divorce her now?"

"Fifty years is sufficient," the brazen servant answered.

Her insolence, rather than repelling him, attracted him the more. Walking to her bed, he sat on the edge. A vile warmth arose from her. Seized by a powerful desire, he said, "How can I divorce her? She won't consent."

"You can get one without her consent," said the servant, apparently well-informed.

Blandishments and promises would not change her mind. To all Nathan's arguments, she turned a deaf ear. Day was already breaking when he returned to his bed. His bedroom walls were gray as canvas. Like a coal glowing on a heap of ashes, the sun arose in the east, casting a light, scarlet as the fire of hell. A crow, alighting on the windowsill, began to caw with its curved black beak, as though trying to announce a piece of bad news. A shudder went through Nathan's bones. He felt that he was his own master no longer, that the Evil Spirit, having seized the reins, drove him along an iniquitous path, perilous and full of obstacles.

From then on Nathan did not have a moment's respite.

While his wife, Roise Temerl, observed the mourning period for her sister in Janow, he was roused each night, and driven to Shifra Zirel, who, each time, rejected him.

Begging and imploring, he promised valuable gifts, offered a rich dowry and inclusion in his will, but nothing availed him. He vowed not to return to her, but his vow was broken each time. He spoke foolishly, in a manner unbecoming to a respectable man, and disgraced himself. When he woke her, she not only chased him away, but scolded him. In passing from his room to hers in the darkness, he would stumble against doors, cupboards, stoves, and he was covered with bruises. He ran into a slop basin and spilled it. He shattered glassware. He tried to recite a chapter of the Psalms that he knew by heart and implored God to rescue him from the net I had spread, but the holy words were distorted on his lips and his mind was confused with impure thoughts. In his bedroom there was a constant buzz and hum from the glowworms, flies, moths, and mosquitoes with which I, the Evil One, had filled it. With eyes open and ears intent, Nathan lay wide awake, listening to each rustle. Roosters crowed, frogs croaked in the swamps, crickets chirped, flashes of lightning glowed strangely. A little imp kept reminding him: Don't be a fool, Reb Nathan, she's waiting for you; she wants to see if you're a man

or a mouse. And the imp hummed: Elul or no
Elul, a woman's a woman, and if you don't enjoy
her in this world it's too late in the next. Nathan
would call Shifra Zirel and wait for her to answer. It seemed to him that he heard the patter
of bare feet, that he saw the whiteness of her
body or of her slip in the darkness. Finally,
trembling, afire, he would rise from his bed to
go to her room. But she remained stubborn.
"Either I or the mistress," she would declare.
"Go, master!"

And grabbing a broom from the pile of refuse,
she would smack him across the back. Then Reb
Nathan Jozefover, the richest man in Frampol,
respected by young and old, would return de-
feated and whipped to his canopied bed, to toss
feverishly until sunrise.

V

Forest Road

Roise Temerl, when she returned from Janow
and saw her husband, was badly frightened. His
face was ashen; there were bags under his eyes;
his beard, which until recently had been black,
was now threaded with white; his stomach had
become loose, and hung like a sack. Like one
dangerously ill, he could barely drag his feet
along. "Woe is me, even finer things than this
are put in the grave!" she exclaimed. She began

to question him, but since he could not tell her the truth, he said he was suffering from headaches, heartburn, stitches, and similar ailments. Roise Temerl, though she had looked forward to seeing her husband and had hoped to enjoy herself with him, ordered a carriage and horses and told him to see a doctor in Lublin. Filling a suitcase with cookies, jams, juices, and various other refreshments, she urged him not to spare money, but to find the best doctors and to take all the medication he prescribed. Shifra Zirel too, saw her master depart, escorting the carriage on foot as far as the bridge, and wishing him a speedy recovery.

Late at night, by the light of the full moon, while the carriage drove along a forest road and shadows ran ahead, I, the Evil Spirit, came to Reb Nathan and asked, "Where are you going?"

"Can't you see? To a doctor."

"Your ailment can't be cured by a doctor," I said.

"What shall I do then? Divorce my old wife?"

"Why not?" I said to him, "Did not Abraham drive his bondwoman, Hagar, into the wilderness, with nothing but a bottle of water, because he preferred Sarah? And later, did he not take Keturah and have six sons with her? Did not Moses, the teacher of all Jews, take, in addition to Zipporah, another wife from the land of Kush; and when Miriam, his sister, spoke against him, did she not become leprous? Know ye, Nathan, you are fated to have sons and daughters, and according to the law, you should have divorced Roise Temerl ten years after marrying her? Well, you may not leave the world without begetting children, and Heaven, therefore, has sent you Shifra Zirel to lie in your lap and become pregnant and bear healthy children, who after your death, will say *kaddish* for you and will inherit your possessions. Therefore do not try to resist, Nathan, for such is the decree of Heaven, and if you do not execute it, you will be punished, you will die soon, and Roise Temerl will be a widow anyway and you will inherit hell."

Hearing these words, Nathan became frightened. Shuddering from head to foot, he said, "If so, why do I go to Lublin? I should, rather, order the driver to return to Frampol."

And I replied, "No, Nathan. Why tell your wife what you're about to do? When she learns you plan to divorce her and take the servant in her place, she will be greatly grieved, and may revenge herself on you or the servant. Rather follow the advice Shifra Zirel gave you. Get divorce papers in Lublin and place them secretly in your wife's dresses; this will make the divorce valid. Then tell her that doctors had advised you to go to Vienna for an operation since you have an internal growth. And before leaving, collect all the money and take it along with you, leaving your wife only the house and the fur-

niture and her personal belongings. Only when
you are far from home, and Shifra Zirel with
you, you may inform Roise Temerl that she is
a divorcee. In this way you will avoid scandal.
But do not delay, Nathan, for Shifra Zirel won't
tarry, and if she leaves you, you might be punished and perish and lose this world as well as
the next."

I made more speeches, pious and impious, and
at daybreak, when he fell asleep, I brought him
Shifra Zirel, naked, and showed him the images
of the children she would bear, male and female,
with side whiskers and curls, and I made him
eat imaginary dishes she had prepared for him:
they tasted of Paradise. He awoke from these
visions, famished, and consumed with desire.
Approaching the city, the carriage stopped at
an inn, where Nathan was served breakfast and
a soft bed prepared for him. But on his palate
there remained the savor of the pancake he had
tasted in his dream. And on his lips he could
almost feel Shifra Zirel's kisses. Overcome with
longing, he put on his coat again, and told his
hosts he must hurry to meet merchants.

In a back alley where I led him, he discovered
a miserly scribe, who for five gulden, wrote the
divorce papers and had them signed by witnesses, as required by law. Then Nathan, after
purchasing numerous bottles and pills from an
apothecary, returned to Frampol. He told his
wife he had been examined by three doctors,

that they had all found he had a tumor in his stomach, and that he must go at once to Vienna to be treated by great specialists or he would not last the year. Shaken by the story, Roise Temerl said, "What's money? Your health means far more to me." She wanted to accompany him, but Nathan reasoned with her and argued, "The trip will cost double; moreover, our business here must be looked after. No, stay here, and God willing, if everything goes well, I'll be back, we'll be happy together." To make a long story short, Roise Temerl agreed with him and stayed.

The same night, after Roise Temerl had fallen asleep, Nathan rose from bed and quietly placed the divorce papers in her trunk. He also visited Shifra Zirel in her room to inform her of what he had done. Kissing and embracing him, she promised to be a good wife and faithful mother to his children. But in her heart, jeering, she though: You old fool, you'll pay dearly for falling in love with a whore.

And now starts the story of how I and my companions forced the old sinner, Nathan Jozefover, to become a man who sees without being seen, so that his bones would never be properly buried, which is the penalty for lechery.

VI

Nathan Returns

A year passed, Roise Temerl now had a second husband, having married a Frampol grain dealer, Moshe Mecheles, who had lost his wife at the same time as she had been divorced. Moshe Mecheles was a small red-bearded man, with heavy red eyebrows and piercing yellow eyes. He often disputed with the Frampol rabbi, put on two pairs of phylacteries while praying, and owned a water mill. He was always covered with white flour dust. He had been rich before, and after his marriage to Roise Temerl, he took over her granaries and customers and became a magnate.

Why had Roise Temerl married him? For one thing, other people intervened. Secondly, she was lonely, and thought that another husband might at least partially replace Nathan. Third, I, the Seducer, had my own reasons for wanting her married. Well, after marrying, she realized she had made a mistake. Moshe Mecheles had odd ways. He was thin, and she tried to fatten him, but he would not touch her dumplings, pancakes, and chickens. He preferred bread with garlic, potatoes in their skins, onions and radishes, and once a day, a piece of lean boiled beef. His stained caftan was never buttoned; he wore a string to hold up his trousers, refused

to go to the bath Roise Temerl would heat for
him, and had to be forced to change a shirt or
a pair of underpants. Moreover he was rarely
at home; he either traveled for business or attended community meetings. He went to sleep
late, and groaned and snored in his bed. When
the sun rose, so did Moshe Mecheles, humming
like a bee. Although close to sixty, Roise Temerl
still did not disdain what others like, but Moshe
Mecheles came to her rarely, and then it was
only a question of duty. The woman finally con-
ceded that she had blundered, but what could
be done? She swallowed her pride and suffered
silently.

One afternoon around Elul time, when Roise
Temerl went to the yard to pour out the slops,
she saw a strange figure. She cried out; the
basin fell from her hands, the slops spilled at
her feet. Ten paces away stood Nathan, her former husband. He was dressed like a beggar, his
caftan torn, a piece of rope around his loins, his
shoes in shreds, and on his head only the lining
of a cap. His once pink face was now yellow, and
the clumps of his beard were gray; pouches
hung from his eyes. From his disheveled eyebrows he stared at Roise Temerl. For a moment
it occurred to her that he must have died, and
this was his ghost before her. She almost called
out: Pure Soul, return to your place of rest! But
since this was happening in broad daylight, she
soon recovered from her shock and asked in a
trembling voice:

"Do my eyes deceive me?"

"No," said Nathan, "It is I."

For a long time husband and wife stood silently gazing at each other. Roise Temerl was so stunned that she could not speak. Her legs began to shake, and she had to hold on to a tree to keep from falling.

"Woe is me, what has become of you?" she cried.

"Is your husband at home?" Nathan asked.

"My husband?" she was bewildered, "no..."

About to ask him in, Roise Temerl remembered that according to law, she was not permitted to stay under the same roof with him. Also, she feared that the servant might recognize him. Bending, she picked up the slop basin.

"What happened?" she asked.

Haltingly, Nathan told her how he had met Shifra Zirel in Lublin, married her, and been persuaded by her to go to her relatives in Hungary. At an inn near the border, she deserted him, stealing everything, even his clothes. Since then, he had wandered all over the country, slept in poorhouses, and like a beggar, made the rounds of private homes. At first he had thought he would obtain a writ signed by one hundred rabbis, enabling him to remarry, and he had set out for Frampol. Then he had learned that Roise Temerl had married again, and he had come to beg her forgiveness.

Unable to believe her eyes, Roise Temerl kept staring at him. Leaning on his crooked stick, as a beggar might, he never lifted his eyes. From his ears and nostrils, thatches of hair protruded. Through his torn coat, she saw the sackcloth, and through a slit in it, his flesh. He seemed to have grown smaller.

"Have any of the townspeople seen you?" she asked.

"No. I came through the fields."

"Woe is me. What can I do with you now?" she exclaimed, "I am married."

"I don't want anything from you," Nathan said, "Farewell."

"Don't go!" Roise Temerl said, "Oh, how unlucky I am!"

Covering her face with her hands, she began to sob. Nathan moved aside.

"Don't mourn for me," he said, "I haven't died yet."

"I wish you had," she replied, "I'd be happier."

Well, I, the Destroyer, had not yet tried all my insidious tricks. The scale of sins and punishment was not yet balanced. Therefore, in a vigorous move, I spoke to the woman in the language of compassion, for it is known that compassion, like any other sentiment, can serve evil as well as good purposes. Roise Temerl, I said, he is your husband; you lived with him for fifty years, and you cannot repudiate him, now that he has fallen. And when she asked, "What shall I do? After all, I cannot stand here and expose myself to derision," I made a suggestion. She trembled, raised her eyes, and beckoned

Nathan to follow her. Submissively, he walked behind her, like any poor visitor who does everything that the lady of the house tells him to do.

VII

The Secret of the Ruin

In the yard, behind the granary, near the bath-house, stood a ruin in which many years before, Roise Temerl's parents had lived. Unoccupied now, its ground floor windows were boarded, but on the second floor there were still a few well preserved rooms. Pigeons perched on the roof, and swallows had nested under the gutter. A worn broom had been stuck in the chimney. Nathan had often said the building should be razed, but Roise Temerl had insisted that while she was alive her parents' home would not be demolished. The attic was littered with old rubbish and rags. Schoolboys said that a light emanated from the ruin at midnight, and that demons lived in the cellar. Roise Temerl led Nathan there now. It was not easy to enter the ruin. Weeds that pricked and burned obstructed the path. Roise Temerl's skirt caught on thorns sharp as nails. Little mole-hills were everywhere. A heavy curtain of cobwebs barred the open doorway. Roise Temerl swept them away with a rotten branch. The stairs were rickety.

Her legs were heavy and she had to lean on
Nathan's arm. A thick cloud of dust arose, and
Nathan began to sneeze and cough.

"Where are you taking me?" he asked, bewildered.

"Don't be afraid," Roise Temerl said, "It's all
right."

Leaving him in the ruin, she returned to the
house. She told the servant to take the rest of
the day off, and the servant did not have to be
told twice. When she had gone, Roise Temerl
opened the cabinets that were still filled with
Nathan's clothes, took his linen from the chest,
and brought everything to the ruin. Once more
she left, and when she returned it was with a
basket containing a meal of rice and pot roast,
tripe with calves' feet, white bread, and stewed
prunes. After he had gobbled his supper and
licked off the prune plate, Roise Temerl drew
a bucket of water from the well and told him
to go to another room to wash. Night was falling, but the twilight lingered a long time. Nathan did as Roise Temerl instructed, and she
could hear him splash and sigh in the next
room. Then he changed his clothes. When Roise
Temerl saw him, tears streamed from her eyes.
The full moon that shone through the window
made the room bright as daylight, and Nathan,
in a clean shirt, his dressing gown embroidered
with leaves and flowers, in his silken cap and
velvet slippers, once again seemed his former
self.

Moshe Mecheles happened to be out of town, and Roise Temerl was in no hurry. She went again to the house and returned with bedding. The bed only needed to be fitted with boards. Not wanting to light a candle, lest someone notice the glow, Roise Temerl went about in the dark, climbed to the attic with Nathan, and groped until she found some old slats for the bed. Then she placed a mattress, sheets, and pillow on it. She had even remembered to bring some jam and a box of cookies so that Nathan could refresh himself before going to sleep. Only then did she sit down on the unsteady stool to rest. Nathan sat on the edge of the bed.

After a long silence, he said, "What's the use? Tomorrow I must leave."

"Why tomorrow?" said Roise Temerl, "Rest up. There's always time to rot in the poorhouse."

Late into the night they sat, talking, murmuring. Roise Temerl cried and stopped crying, began again and was calm again. She insisted that Nathan confess everything to her, without omitting details, and he told her again how he had met Shifra Zirel, how they had married, how she had persuaded him to go with her to Pressburg, and how she had spent the night full of sweet talk and love play with him at an inn. And at daybreak, when he fell asleep, she had arisen and untied the bag from his neck. He also told Roise Temerl how he had been forced to discard all shame, to sleep in beggars' dormitories, and eat at strangers' tables. Although his story angered her, and she called him block-head, stupid fool, ass, idiot, her heart almost dissolved with pity.

"What is there to do now?" she kept mur-muring to herself, over and over again. And I, the Evil Spirit, answered: Don't let him go. The beggar's life is not for him. He might die of grief or shame. And when Roise Temerl argued that because she was a married woman she had no right to stay with him, I said: Can the twelve lines of a bill of divorcement separate two souls who have been fused by fifty years of common life? Can a brother and sister be transformed by law into strangers? Hasn't Nathan become part of you? Don't you see him every night in your dreams? Isn't all your fortune the result of his industry and effort? And what is Moshe Mecheles? A stranger, a lout. Wouldn't it be better to fry with Nathan in hell, rather than serve as Moshe Mecheles' footstool in Heaven? I also recalled to her an incident in a story book, where a landowner, whose wife had eloped with a bear tamer, later forgave her and took her back to his manor.

When the clock in the Frampol church chimed eleven, Roise Temerl returned home. In her lux-urious, canopied bed, she tossed, like one in a fever. For a long time, Nathan stood beside his window, looking out. The Elul sky was full of stars. The owl on the roof of the synagogue screeched with a human voice. The caterwaul-ing of cats reminded him of women in labor.

Crickets chirped, and unseen saws seemed to be buzzing through tree trunks. The neighing of horses that had grazed all night came through the fields with the calls of shepherds. Nathan, because he stood on an upper floor, could see the whole little town at a glance, the synagogue, the church, the slaughterhouse, the public bathhouse, the market, and the side streets where Gentiles lived. He recognized each shed, shack, and board in his own yard. A goat stripped some bark from a tree. A field mouse left the granary to return to its nest. Nathan watched for a long time. Everything about him was familiar and yet strange, real and ghostly, as though he were no longer among the living—only his spirit floated there. He recalled that there was a Hebrew phrase which applied to him, but he could not remember it exactly. Finally, after trying for a long time, he remembered: *one who sees without being seen.*

VIII

One Who Sees Without Being Seen

In Frampol the rumor spread that Roise Temerl, having quarreled with her maid, had dismissed her in the middle of her term. This surprised the housewives, because the girl was reputedly industrious and honest. Actually, Roise Temerl had dismissed the girl to keep her from discovering that Nathan lived in the ruin. As always, when I seduce sinners, I persuaded the couple that all this was provisional, that Nathan would stay only until he had recovered from his wandering. But I made certain that Roise Temerl welcomed the presence of her hidden guest and that Nathan enjoyed being where he was. Even though they discussed their future separation each time they were together, Roise Temerl gave Nathan's quarters an air of permanency. She resumed her cooking and frying for him, and once more brought him her tasty dishes. After a few days, Nathan's appearance changed remarkably. From pastries and puddings, his face became pink again, and once more, like that of a man of wealth, his paunch protruded. Once more he wore embroidered shirts, velvet slippers, silken dressing gowns, and carried batiste handkerchiefs. To keep him from being bored by his idleness, Roise Temerl brought him a Bible in Yiddish, a copy of the *Inheritance of the Deer,* and numerous story books. She even managed to procure some tobacco for his pipe, for he enjoyed smoking one, and she brought from the cellar bottles of wine and mead that Nathan had stored for years. The divorced couple had banquets in the ruin.

I made certain that Moshe Mecheles was seldom at home; I sent him to all kinds of fairs, and even recommended him as arbiter in disputes. It did not take long for the ruin behind the granary to become Roise Temerl's only comfort. Just as a miser's thoughts constantly dwell on the treasure he has buried far from sight, so Roise Temerl thought only of the ruin and the secret in her heart. Sometimes she thought that Nathan had died and she had magically resurrected him for a while; at other times, she imagined the whole thing a dream. Whenever she looked out of her window at the moss-covered roof of the ruin, she thought: No! It's inconceivable for Nathan to be there; I must be deluded. And immediately, she had to fly there, up the rickety stairs, to be met half-way by Nathan in person, with his familiar smile and his pleasant odor. "Nathan, you're here?" she would ask, and he would respond, "Yes, Roise Temerl, I'm here and waiting for you."

"Have you missed me?" she would ask, and he would answer:

"Of course. When I hear your step, it's a holiday for me."

"Nathan, Nathan," she would continue, "Would you have believed a year ago that it would end like this?"

And he would murmur, "No, Roise Temerl, it is like a bad dream."

"Oh Nathan, we have already lost this world, and I'm afraid we'll lose the other also," Roise Temerl said.

And he replied, "Well, that's too bad, but hell too is for people, not for dogs."

Since Moshe Mecheles belonged to the Has-

sidim, I, Old Rebel, sent him to spend the Days
of Awe with his rabbi. Alone, Roise Temerl
bought Nathan a prayer shawl, a white robe,
a prayer book, and prepared a holiday meal for
him. Since on Rosh Hashona, there is no moon,
he ate the evening meal in darkness, blindly
dunked a slice of bread in honey, and tasted an
apple, a carrot, the head of a carp, and offered
a blessing for the first fruit, over a pomegran-
ate. He stood praying during the day in his robe
and prayer shawl. The sound of the ram's horn
came faintly to his ears from the synagogue. At
the intermission between the prayers, Roise
Temerl visited him in her golden dress, her
white, satin-lined coat, and the shawl embroidered with silver threads, to wish him a happy
new year. The golden chain he had given her
for their betrothal hung around her neck. A
brooch he had brought to her from Danzig, quivered on her breast, and from her wrist dangled
a bracelet he had bought her at Brody. She ex-
uded an aroma of honey cake and the women's
section of the synagogue. On the evening before
the Day of Atonement, Roise Temerl brought
him a white rooster as a sacrificial victim and
prepared for him the meal to be eaten before
commencing the fast. Also, she gave the synagogue a wax candle for his soul. Before leaving
for the *Minchah* prayer at the synagogue, she
came to bid him good-by, and she began to la-
ment so loudly that Nathan feared she would

be heard. Falling into his arms, she clung to him and would not be torn away. She drenched his face with tears and howled as though possessed. "Nathan, Nathan," she wailed, "may we have no more unhappiness," and other things that are said when a member of a family dies, repeating them many times. Fearing she might faint and fall, Nathan had to escort her downstairs. Then, standing at the window, he watched the people of Frampol on their way to the synagogue. The women walked quickly and vigorously, as though hurrying to pray for someone on his deathbed; they held up their skirts, and when two of them met, they fell into each other's arms and swayed back and forth as if in some mysterious struggle. Wives of prominent citizens knocked at doors of poor people and begged to be forgiven. Mothers, whose children were ill, ran with arms outstretched, as though chasing someone, crying like madwomen. Elderly men, before leaving home, removed their shoes, put on white robes, prayer shawls, and white skull caps. In the synagogue yard, the poor sat with alms' boxes on benches. A reddish glow spread over the roofs, reflecting in the window panes, and illuminating pale faces. In the west, the sun grew enormous; clouds around it caught fire, until half the sky was suffused with flames. Nathan recalled the River of Fire, in which all souls must cleanse themselves. The sun sank soon below the horizon. Girls, dressed in white, came outside and carefully closed shutters. Little flames played on the high windows of the synagogue, and inside, the entire building seemed to be one great flicker. A muted hum arose from it, and bursts of sobbing. Removing his shoes, Nathan wrapped himself in his shawl and robe. Half reading and half remembering, he chanted the words of Kol Nidre, the song that is recited not only by the living but by the dead in their graves. What was he, Nathan Jozefover, but a dead man, who instead of resting in his grave, wandered about in a world that did not exist?

IX

Footprints in the Snow

The High Holidays were over. Winter had come. But Nathan was still in the ruin. It could not be heated, not only because the stove had been dismantled, but because smoke, coming from the chimney, would make people suspicious. To keep Nathan from freezing, Roise Temerl provided him with warm clothes and a coal pot. At night he covered himself with two feather quilts. During the day he wore his fox fur and had felt boots on his feet. Roise Temerl also brought him a little barrel of spirits with a straw in it, which he sipped each time he felt cold, while eating a piece of dried mutton. From the rich food with which Roise Temerl plied him, he grew fat and heavy. In the evenings he stood at the window watching with curiosity the women who went to the ritual bath. On market days he never left the window. Carts drove into the yard and peasants unloaded sacks of grain. Moshe Mecheles, in a cotton padded jacket, ran back and forth, crying out hoarsely. Although it pained Nathan to think that this ridiculous fellow disposed of his possessions and lay with his wife, Moshe Mecheles' appearance made him laugh, as though the whole thing were a kind of prank that he, Nathan, had played on his competitor. Sometimes he felt like calling to him: Hey, there, Moshe Mecheles! while throwing him a bit of plaster or a bone.

As long as there was no snow, Nathan had everything he needed. Roise Temerl visited him often. At night Nathan would go out for a walk on a path that led to the river. But one night a great deal of snow fell, and the next day Roise Temerl did not visit him, for she was afraid someone might notice her tracks in the snow. Nor could Nathan go out to satisfy his natural needs. For two days he had nothing warm to eat, and the water in the pail turned to ice. On the third day Roise Temerl hired a peasant to clear the snow between the house and the granary and she also told him to clear the snow between the granary and the ruin. Moshe Mecheles, when he came home was surprised and asked, "Why?", but she changed the subject, and since he suspected nothing, he soon forgot about it.

Nathan's life, from then on, became increasingly difficult. After each new snowfall, Roise Temerl cleared the path with a shovel. To keep her neighbors from seeing what went on in the yard, she had the fence repaired. And as a pretext for going to the ruin, she had a ditch for refuse dug close to it. Whenever she saw Nathan, he said it was time for him to take his bundle and leave, but Roise Temerl prevailed on him to wait. "Where will you go?" she asked. "You might, God forbid, drop from exhaustion." According to the almanac, she argued, the winter would be a mild one, and summer would begin early, weeks before Purim, and he only had to get through half the month of Kislev, besides Teveth and Shevat. She told him other things. At times, they did not even speak, but sat silently, holding hands and weeping. Both of them were actually losing strength each day. Nathan grew fatter, more blown up; his belly was full of wind; his legs seemed leaden; and his sight was dimming. He could no longer read his story books. Roise Temerl grew thin, like a consumptive, lost her appetite, and could not sleep. Some nights she lay awake, sobbing. And when Moshe Mecheles asked her why, she said it was because she had no children to pray for her after she was gone.

One day a downpour washed away the snow. Since Roise Temerl had not visited the ruin for two days, Nathan expected her to arrive at any moment. He had no food left; only a bit of brandy remained at the bottom of the barrel. For hours on end he stood waiting for her at the window, which was misted over with frost, but she did not come. The night was pitch black and icy. Dogs barked, a wind blew. The walls of the ruin shook; a whistling sound ran through the chimney, and the eaves rattled on the roof. In Nathan's house, now the house of Moshe Mecheles, several lamps seemed to have been lighted; it seemed extraordinarily bright, and the light made the surrounding darkness thicker. Nathan thought he heard the rolling of wheels, as though a carriage had driven to the house. In the darkness, someone drew water from the well, and someone poured out the slops. The night wore on, but despite the late hour, the shutters remained open. Seeing shadows run back and forth, Nathan thought important visitors might have come and were being treated to a banquet. He remained staring into the night until his knees grew weak, and with his last bit of strength, he dragged himself to his bed and fell into a deep sleep.

The cold awoke him early next morning. With stiff limbs he arose and barely propelled himself to the window. More snow had fallen during the night, and a heavy frost had set in.

To his amazement, Nathan saw a group of men and women standing around his house. He wondered, anxiously, what was going on. But he did not have to wonder long, for suddenly the door swung open, and four men carried out a coffin hearse covered with a black cloth. "Moshe Mecheles is dead!" Nathan thought. But then he saw Moshe Mecheles following the coffin. It was not he, but Roise Temerl who had died.

Nathan could not weep. It was as though the cold had frozen his tears. Trembling and shaking, he watched the men carrying the coffin, watched the beadle rattling his alms box and the mourners wading through deep snowdrifts. The sky, pale as linen, hung low, meeting the blanketed earth. As though drifting on a flood, the trees in the fields seemed to be afloat in whiteness. From his window, Nathan could see all the way to the cemetery. The coffin moved up and down; the crowd, following it, thinned out and at times vanished entirely, seemed to sink into the ground and then emerge again. Nathan fancied for a moment that the cortege had stopped and no longer advanced, and then, that the people, as well as the corpse, were moving backward. The cortege grew gradually smaller, until it became a black dot. Because the dot ceased to move, Nathan realized that the pall bearers had reached the cemetery, and that he was watching his faithful wife being buried. With the remaining brandy, he washed

his hands, for the water in his pail had turned
to ice, and he began to murmur the prayer for
the dead.

X

Two Faces

Nathan had intended to pack his things and
leave during the night, but I, the Chief of the
devils, prevented him from carrying out his
plan. Before sunrise he was seized with powerful stomach cramps; his head grew hot and
his knees so weak that he could not walk. His
shoes had grown brittle; he could not put them
on; and his legs had become fat. The Good Spirit
counseled him to call for help, to shout until
people heard and came to rescue him, because
no man may cause his own death, but I said to
him: Do you remember the words of King David:
"Let me rather fall into God's hands, than into
the hands of people?" You don't want Moshe
Mecheles and his henchmen to have the satisfaction of revenging themselves on you and jeering. Rather die like a dog. In short, he listened
to me, first, because he was proud, and second,
because he was not fated to be buried according
to law.

Gathering together his last remnants of
strength, he pushed his bed to the window, to
lie there and watch. He fell asleep early and

awoke. There was day, and then night. Sometimes he heard cries in the yard. At other times he thought someone called him by name. His head, he fancied, had grown monstrously large and burdensome, like a millstone carried on his neck. His fingers were wooden, his tongue hard; it seemed bigger than the space it occupied. My helpers, goblins, appeared to him in dreams. They screamed, whistled, kindled fires, walked on stilts, and carried on like Purim players. He dreamed of floods, then of fires, imagined the world had been destroyed, and then that he hovered in the void with bats' wings. In his dreams he also saw pancakes, dumplings, broad noodles with cheese, and when he awoke his stomach was as full as though he had actually eaten; he belched and sighed, and touched his belly that was empty and aching all over.

Once, sitting up, he looked out of the window, and saw to his surprise that people were walking backward, and marveled at this. Soon he saw other extraordinary things. Among those who passed, he recognized men who had long been dead. "Do my eyes deceive me?" he wondered, "Or has Messiah come, and has he resurrected the dead?" The more he looked the more astonished he became. Entire generations passed through the town, men and women with packs on their shoulders and staffs in their hands. He recognized, among them, his father and grandfather, his grandmothers and great-aunts. He watched workers build the Frampol synagogue. They carried bricks, sawed wood, mixed plaster, nailed on eaves. Schoolboys stood about, staring upward and calling a strange word he could not understand, like something in a foreign tongue. As in a dance around the Torah, two storks circled the building. Then the building and builders vanished, and he saw a group of people, barefooted, bearded, wild-eyed, with crosses in their hands, lead a Jew to the gallows. Though the black-bearded young man cried heart-rendingly, they dragged him on, tied in ropes. Bells were ringing; the people in the streets ran away and hid. It was midday, but it grew dark as the day of an eclipse of the sun. Finally, the young man cried out: "Shema Yisroel, the Lord our God, the Lord is One," and was left hanging, his tongue lolling out. His legs swayed for a long time, and hosts of crows flew overhead, cawing hoarsely.

On his last night, Nathan dreamed that Roise Temerl and Shifra Zirel were one woman with two faces. He was overjoyed at her appearance. "Why have I not noticed this before?" he wondered. "Why did I have to go through this trouble and anxiety?" He kissed the two-faced female, and she returned his kisses with her doubled lips, pressing against him her two pairs of breasts. He spoke words of love to her, and she responded in two voices. In her four arms and two bosoms, all his questions were answered. There was no longer life and death, here nor there, beginning nor end. "The truth is twofold," Nathan exclaimed, "This is the mystery of all mysteries!"

Without a last confession of his sins, Nathan died that night. I at once transported his soul to the nether abyss. He still wanders to this day in desolate spaces, and has not yet been granted admittance to hell. Moshe Mecheles married again, a young woman this time. She made him pay dearly, soon inherited his fortune, and squandered it. Shifra Zirel became a harlot in Pressburg and died in the poorhouse. The ruin still stands as before, and Nathan's bones still lie there. And, who can tell, perhaps another man, who sees without being seen, is hiding in it.

Translated by Norbert Guterman
and Elaine Gottlieb

A NOTE ABOUT THE AUTHOR

Isaac Bashevis Singer was born in Rad-
zymin, Poland, in 1904 and grew up in
Warsaw. He emigrated to the United States
in 1935. Among his works are the autobio-
graphical memoir *In My Father's Court*,
and the novels *The Family Moskat*, *The
Magician of Lublin*, and *Enemies, A Love
Story*. His short story collections include
Gimpel the Fool, *Short Friday*, and *A
Crown of Feathers*. On being awarded the
Nobel Prize for Literature, he was cited for
his "impassioned narrative art which, with
roots in a Polish-Jewish cultural tradition,
brings the universal human condition to
life."